KATE WILD

Chicken House

Scholastic Inc./New York

Text copyright © 2007 by Kate Wild

First published in the United Kingdom in 2007 by Chicken House,
2 Palmer Street, Frome, Somerset BA11 1DS. *www.doublecluck.com*

Library of Congress Cataloging-in-Publication Data

Wild, Kate, 1971- Fight game / by Kate Wild. — 1st American ed. p. cm.
Summary: Fifteen-year-old Freedom Smith is a fighter, just like all of
his relatives who have the "Hercules gene," which leads him to a choice
between being jailed for attempted murder or working with a covert law
enforcement agency to break up a mysterious, illegal fight ring.

ISBN 13: 978-0-439-87175-4 · ISBN 10: 0-439-87175-1

[1. Hand-to-hand fighting—Fiction. 2. Spies—Fiction. 3. Undercover
operations—Fiction. 4. Genetic engineering—Fiction. 5. Science fiction.]
I. Title.

PZ7.W645732Fig 2007
[Fic]—dc22

2006032889

10 9 8 7 6 5 4 3 2 1   07 08 09 10 11

Printed in the U.S.A.   23

First American edition, July 2007
The text type was set in EideticNeo.
The display type was set in Flyerfonts and ChollaSans.
Book design by Leyah Jensen

This book is dedicated
to the

SOURCE
OF ALL EVIL
CLAN

—————————

And thanks to

Julia,
Imogen, and
Barry

MISSING PERSON

Johnny Sparrow
17 years old

Last seen in this area wearing a blue
sweatshirt with an All England Karate Squad
logo, jeans, and sneakers.

Anyone with information should contact
01733 4592321

I was halfway down the drainpipe, hanging on for dear life. I couldn't go any farther because there was a policewoman down below, nailing a poster to the wall. I'd seen the same thing pinned up all over town, asking for information about this Johnny guy.

It was past midnight, so it was just my bad luck to run into the policewoman. And even though I swear to God I wasn't up to anything bad, it didn't look good for a Gypsy boy to be shinning down the nineteenth-century drainpipe of the cathedral.

I'd been up on the roof, but only so's I could sit on the highest ledge and eat my takeout Chicken Balti and Peshwari Nan with only the gargoyles and the stars for company. This combined my two favorite pastimes: climbing the highest thing I can find and eating chilies. But you can bet that if the policewoman saw me coming down, she'd think I'd been up there after the lead or something.

I'd got a good grip on the pipe, the sort monkeys use on tree trunks when they're climbing. It meant my feet acting like another pair of hands, so I could hold on for a while longer without moving, but not forever. I was already losing the skin on my palms to the rusted iron of the pipe. So to take my mind off my predicament, I began thinking about what my mammy'd do if I got lost. I don't think she'd sit back and rely on posters; traveler kids are like little princes and princesses. If you don't believe me just go to a Gypsy wedding and see them all in their D&G Junior, with their mammies and daddies watching them with doting eyes. Gypsy families are so close-knit, there's never a chance to stray.

I shifted my grip slightly. Another cop had joined the policewoman and they were standing talking. Jeez, didn't they have any crooks to chase?

"Johnny Sparrow? Is he one of the Sparowski Corporation Sparrows?" said the cop, nodding at the poster.

"Yep, the only son," said the policewoman. "Ran away from boarding school. Last seen living rough near the park. Poor little rich boy, right?"

I let go with one hand and shook it to get some life back in it. This Johnny Sparrow should have been a traveler boy – then he wouldn't have had to run away from school. I'm almost sixteen and I've hardly seen the inside of a school since I was eleven. At eleven we go out with our dads and learn something useful like a trade, instead of sitting behind a desk all day long. It's not that our parents don't want us educated: If we could afford private tutors, then I swear we'd all have degrees and letters after our names. They just don't like us out of their sight. As I said, we don't get lost, not like this Johnny Sparrow.

There was a *crack* and the nineteenth-century pipe left the wall by a couple of inches. Bits of brick showered down. I made myself light. I swear, if I'm desperate enough I can nearly hover when I want to. It's not magic, it's how you spread your weight; just a tiny movement can shift the balance in your favor. It's a monkey thing again; just watch them, they're the masters.

"What the hell –?" The cop brushed brick dust from his shoulder.

"What's up?"

"Thought I heard something up there."

I froze. The cop was squinting up through the darkness. If he shone a flashlight, he'd see me straightaway. The world stopped and my fate hung in the balance. All that happened after that – my life getting tangled with Johnny's, the girl, the cops, and the fighting – none of it would have happened if he'd shone his flashlight upward. My life was at a crossroads, but I didn't know it then.

"Want to check it out?"

"Nah, let's go and visit All-Night Ned's and get a cuppa."

The world started spinning again, and my path was set. I gave it a couple of minutes, then dropped down the last twenty feet or so and legged it back to the trailers, taking the scenic route – which meant running along walls and across low roofs and not touching the ground at all. It might be dangerous, but it's my preferred method of crossing town. I blame it on one of my ancestors, a fighting man by the name of Hercules Smith. He's the reason I'm a freak.

||

One hundred fifty years ago my great-great-great-granddaddy, Hercules Smith, was a champion of the fairground fighting booths. By the time he was twenty he'd beaten all the best fighters: Gentleman Jim, The Sledgehammer, Jack the Knife, and even Granite Tom. After that, he made mincemeat of Queen Victoria's favorites, Davy "Welsh Terrier" Jones and the London Hornet. He could go ninety rounds even with his knuckles split and his legs giving way. He just wouldn't go down no matter what, and no fighter could stop him.

And it wasn't just in the ring that he was unbeatable. No one could stop him in life, either. He could run from the cops, swerving like a lurcher after a hare, and he could go up drainpipes like a rat. They say he knew the roofs of a town better than he knew the streets below. Eventually they tried hanging him for horse thieving just to slow him down, but he escaped even that.

Then, for the next century and a half, Hercules' sons, and then their sons, became bare-knuckle fighters in their own right. And so it went on, each son stronger than the last, until the Smith fighters had sinews of

5

steel and bones made of granite and minds that could switch to reptile thinking at a moment's notice.

"If you want to fight like Hercules, you've got to use your reptile brain," my daddy used to tell us. "A crocodile's got only one concern, survival. Kick him and he'll bite back without a second thought. He doesn't hold a grudge, his brain just goes, *Someone kicked me! Bite!*"

Hercules' reptile thinking was what made the Smiths unbeatable.

But it wasn't the only thing. In each generation a boy would be born who could punch harder and run faster and had reflexes quicker than greased lightning. And sometimes these champion Smiths led long lives full of sporting glory, even though it was an illegal behind-closed-doors glory. But usually they led short fast lives that ended with them dancing on the end of a rope.

Now I'm the one to wear that particular crown. I'm Freedom Hercules Smith, the only one ever named after the old fighter, and I don't know whether I'm going to end up with the glory, but it wasn't looking very good for me.

There was a problem, see.

There didn't seem to be a use for boys like me anymore. I was growing up, and getting too big and too troublesome. But was I going to be like Uncle Shady, a bare-knuckle fighter with a cauliflower ear, a nose like a squashed tomato, and the shakes from getting one too many knocks to his head? Or was I going to be like

Granddaddy Bartley Smith, a rogue? They say the local prison kept a cell ready for him, he was in and out so often. Or would I sell out like some of us, and go and live in a house and get a job working for someone?

A sideshow, a sellout, or a crook. Was that it?

The truth was, I'd fight forever for my family, and no one could stop me when I really got going – not even my daddy, even though he was a champ in his day, too. The last time we had a row I ended up coming to live with my sister, so that we weren't near each other anymore.

And what did the police tell me every time I got into trouble?

They said fighting was wrong and I must go to school.

Fat chance.

● ● ●

When I got back from my expedition on the cathedral roof, I found that a skinhead had spray-painted BURN THE PIKEYS on the side of my sister's home. It seemed they didn't like it because it was a home on wheels and parked on spare ground.

Worst of all, my little nieces saw it and asked me what it said. So I put on my clown act and said, "Don't worry, it's just some bad guys. They've gone now. They won't be coming back."

And I kept my fingers crossed behind my back,

because if the bad guys did come back I'd deal with them, but not while the girls were around.

"If they did, would you get 'em for us, Fwed?" said little Whitney Jade, reading my mind. "Would you be a deadeye knight?"

"It's *Jedi* Knight, and 'course I would. You don't ever need to fear anybody in all your lives," I said quietly, so no one would hear.

"Leave it, Fred," said my sister, who's got ears like a hare's. "You know what the police told you. Leave it or you'll get into trouble." She looked away and then back. "Old Hercules' strength is like a curse to the Smiths. Nothing good ever comes of it."

And in the back of my mind all I kept thinking was: *I wish someone would stop me.* But that's the problem. There was no one.

"I'm burning inside about it and my fists are itching," I said to her. Crystal understands me sometimes. She's inherited some of the Smith fighting spirit as well. But this time she grabbed my chin and made me look at her.

"Leave it. Mammy'll break her heart if you go to prison."

"OK." But I knew I'd go back on my word.

And I did, that very night.

|||

I was stretched out like a cat and just as silent.

Our little campsite was bathed in moonlight. We were on a bit of spare ground between two factories, the remains of our campfire smoldering in the still summer air. It wasn't long after midnight, the unholy hour when trouble always brews. The air was still warm after a scorching hot day, and now there was a smell of thunder in the air. But the only things disturbing the silence of the night were a couple of flitting shadows and the sound of two people breathing as quietly as possible.

"You got the spray paint?" whispered one.

"I've got more than that!" came the reply.

One shadow moved and then the other, silently surveying the site. Then the two shapes retreated under the old conker tree growing out of the tarmac by the entrance to the parking lot.

There was a small pop, like a cork being pulled from an already opened bottle of wine, and then a potent scent blossomed in the air.

Gasoline. It smelled like hatred.

"Jesus Christ, Clunk!" said the first whisperer, the

one who thought he was here to do another paint job on the trailer. "Are you crazy?"

Yes, I'd say he was crazy. Anyone with a nickname like Clunk couldn't have much up top.

"We warned 'em," said Clunk, in a whisper that turned my spine to ice. "And they didn't move." He spat on the ground. "Anyway, that cocky kid needs teaching a lesson."

Me, presumably.

"I've seen him strutting around acting tough," said Clunk, and spat again.

The spray paint had obviously just been a warning. Now Clunk, who must have been watching our peaceful little camp, was going to stage two. Or so he thought.

"I'm out of here!" said his friend, but I saw Clunk grab him by his hooded top.

"Stay where you are, kid. You're in this now whether you want it or not."

They were close together now. It couldn't have been more perfect. I rolled from the conker tree's branch and dropped on them like an avenging angel.

"Sorry, didn't ruin anything, did I?" I said, but for the moment they weren't listening. They were on the ground, winded and trying to clear their heads. The bottle of gas flew through the air and landed on the smoldering campfire. With a soft *whump* it burst into flames, illuminating the arena for me.

By the flickering light of the flames I had a split second to decide who to tackle first, the leader or the follower. The one who's the boss and calling the shots can be dangerous, but a follower can be just as bad. Some people will become saints if they follow a good man, but will outdo the devil if they hitch up with a bad guy.

The one in the hooded sweatshirt was the first to get groggily to his feet, so I made my decision. I left Clunk, who was still winded on the ground, and squared up to meet Hoodie.

Funnily enough, without his friend he didn't seem to want to square up to me.

"OK, this is all a mistake!" he said, and I could hear the fear in his voice. I think he hadn't recovered from the shock of seeing Clunk brandish a Molotov cocktail followed by me appearing from nowhere.

"Shh! Keep your voice down!" I whispered, bouncing backward. "We don't want the gavvers, do we?"

"The what?" he mumbled, stumbling toward me. But I moved farther back again. I don't think he'd got all his wits yet, because he hadn't worked out I was trying to edge him farther away from the trailers.

"Gavvers, police, cops, it's all the same," I said, still moving lightly on my toes away from him. To tell you the truth, it was my sister's baby I didn't want him disturbing. Jeez, if that little terror woke up, he'd squawk the place down. Then my sister'd come out and she'd probably do more damage to Hoodie than me, because Little Frisco could cry for England when woken up.

I was still dancing back, keeping out of his way, when he got his courage back and lunged forward, punching me on the shoulder. I think he'd got the impression that I couldn't fight back, that I was retreating out of fear. He didn't know that to me the art of fighting is *not* fighting – until you really have to. On good days I believe this is because underneath it all I'm honorable. But on bad days I think it's because, maybe, I won't know how to stop.

He'd got his hood pulled well up over his head so's I couldn't see his face, couldn't read his thoughts, which is important in a fight. But he was a trier, I'll give him that. Here he was now, getting into a fancy karate position and ghost-walking toward me.

Ghost-walking, God help him! I could almost hear the ghost of old Hercules saying, "What the devil is he doing that for? Just kick him in the vulnerables and be done with all this fancy nonsense!"

But I didn't do that. I just bounced back a bit more, and let him expend more of his energy.

"Scared to face me, huh?" he said, breaking into my thoughts. And he punched me hard on the jaw. Which just goes to show, never start thinking deeply in the middle of a fight. In fact, don't think at all, just go with your reptile brain, like old Hercules recommended. So I did. For the first time I put my fists up and I fixed him in my sight.

I've got an ugly mug and I look even worse when I'm scowling. And with the flickering flames of the campfire casting shadows over my face as well, I probably looked like the devil's apprentice. He took one look at me and froze, now that he'd got the fight he'd been asking for.

His problem was that he was a follower, a plus-one. I think he was waiting for the referee to say, "Go," or for his girlfriend to say, "Leave 'im, love, he ain't worth it!" or for his mate to pull him back by the hood of his sweatshirt. He took one look at my fists and the look in my eye, and he backed off a little. I was glad of it; things were getting too noisy. So I swung a huge slow punch toward him and let him dodge it, to give him a bit of encouragement. It worked; he saw his chance and raced by me, and then he disappeared into the balmy night.

It was good he'd done a runner because my real enemy, the skinhead called Clunk, had now leaped to his feet and was coming at me from behind.

This one was trained, and trained well. But whoever had trained him shouldn't have, because he was the unstable pup, the one that'd bite anyone, friend or foe, if he was in the mood. Not only that, he was superfueled by high-octane hatred. He didn't need a hood to hide his face because he knew that no one who saw his face, when he didn't want it seen, would be in a fit state to pick him out of a police lineup.

He came at me like a pit bull after the neighbor's cat. He expected me to take a big swing at him, but I sidestepped to off-balance him and he tripped and fell. But he was back up in seconds and coming at me again. He knew his stuff; he went for the center line where the pressure points are, so I let him punch me for a few seconds, then feinted to the left as though I'd stumbled from his blows. He was running on hatred so he wasn't thinking clearly, or he'd have known what I was doing. But just for that split second he let down his guard, thinking I was going to fall. That was my chance. I tripped him again, and this time I leaped onto his back while he was still flat out. Then I got his arm into a lock.

"Murderer. You were going to set fire to the trailer." I was speaking close to his ear, to keep the noise down, but I think he could hear the disbelief in my voice. I still couldn't believe that anyone would plan anything so evil.

He grunted and then got his face out of the ground. "You got it all wrong," he panted. "I was just going to give you a warning, just going to set fire to your Dumpster, see." He tried to turn around, but I pulled his arm back. "Honest, kid."

I hesitated when he said that. I think I wanted to believe that nobody hated us so much they'd set fire to our trailer. As I hesitated he must have felt me loosen my grip ever so slightly, and boy, was he quick. In a split

14

second he'd twisted around and I heard the *shtik* of a knife unfolding, and I saw a flash of moonlight on the blade as he aimed at my face. I couldn't dodge it, he'd follow any move I made, so I palmed him hard on his other shoulder and his aim was knocked wide, but I still felt the blade cut me.

That was the thing that finished it, the feeling of blood on my arm. I had a flashback to the bad dream I keep having – a black car in the dead of night, a man in the shadows, a sharp pain in my arm, but nothing more, no explanation. Jeez, the times I've woken up sweating from that dream.

But I didn't have time to worry about it now. The smell of gas on Clunk wiped out everything else. In my mind's eye the firebomb flew and my little nieces screamed. He might have been fueled by hatred, but now all I could see was the vision of an orange fireball inside a trailer. It was time to jive.

"You ever seen a trailer burn?" I said softly, in between taking deep breaths to push extra oxygen into my muscles. Some people start shouting when they're really angry; I just get quieter, but it's a deadly sort of quiet. I save my breath for the fight.

"It goes up like a firework, even if there's no gas bottles exploding, and in about five minutes it's a metal frame and a puddle of molten rubber from the tires." I moved forward; I don't think even a truck could have stopped me now.

"If you were in a trailer that went up, you wouldn't stand a chance, I swear to God you wouldn't," I told him, circling as he tried to jab out and get me. He'd no chance, I was too quick. "It'd be a red-hot metal skeleton before the fire engine even got out of the station."

Then I'd had enough talking and I put up my fists. I don't know what sort of look I had on my face, maybe he thought I'd gone crazy, maybe he could even see the red fire of the burning trailer in my eyes. I don't know, but big as he was, he took one look at my face and turned and ran.

That's when I did a wrong thing. I ran after him. Away from the trailers we went, like bats out of hell. Out onto the road. I think I saw it first, the late-night bus. Sure as hell he didn't see it.

I know I dived. I know that much. That was never in dispute.

But did I dive to push him out into the road, as Hoodie claimed later? Or did I dive to drag him out of the way, as I said I did? Was I a devil or an angel? It didn't really matter, because the bus hit him and he rolled and lay still.

||||

Show me around a town once and I'll remember the street plan in my head forever. Give me your phone number and I won't have to write it down, I'll just file it in my head. It's the same with faces.

I'd seen Hoodie's face as we waited for the ambulance to come. I wouldn't forget in a hurry the look on his face. And I didn't think I'd ever forget Clunk's. I'd go to my grave with that image. They did what they could for him as he lay on the road, and then strung him up to drips and monitors and wheeled him away on a stretcher.

It was almost dawn by this time; the sky was lightening and the air had gone chilly as it always does just before the sun rises, even in the middle of a heat wave. They questioned Hoodie and me separately, then they told me to go into the trailer, and they left a cop in a car outside as the sun rose.

For the next hour, as I lay in my bunk unable to close my eyes, a videotape played and replayed in my head of the few seconds it took Clunk to run across the road and get hit by the bus. Over and over it went, on a loop in my head, and there was nothing I could do to stop it.

Crystal and Joe had woken when the ambulance arrived, and they'd come out and stood by me. The little girls never heard a thing that night, but in the morning they knew something was wrong.

"You keep quiet about it," said Crystal, poking me hard in the chest with her spoon. Jeez, it's not only the boys who get the sinews of steel in the Smith family.

We were sitting outside the trailers on the patio chairs, trying to have breakfast. The traffic was thundering by on the other side of the parking lot, but it didn't disturb us. Even when we're on an official traveler site, they're always built by a highway or a railway line. It's a wonder traveler kids ever grow up, what with all the pollution.

I was keeping my eye on the bus stop and the row of boys waiting by it. My reptile senses hadn't shut down yet, and the whole world seemed to be a threat.

I'd given up trying to eat. Hoodie's punch last night had swollen the inside of my mouth and I kept accidentally biting my cheek. It was driving me crazy because I couldn't stop touching it with my tongue.

Whitney Jade, covered in Coco Pops, said, "I dreamed you was fighting, Fwed."

"Gnuh?" I tried to look innocent, but it's a bit difficult when you're secretly inspecting the results of a fight.

"There was a nee-naa in the night," she insisted. That's what she calls an ambulance.

"There was nothing, baby girl." I leaned back in my

chair to get in the shade. Even this early the air felt like it had been heated in an oven. I'd got a tight feeling in my head, too; either thunder was on the way, or it was a warning of more trouble to come.

She pointed to my arm. "You're bleeding, Fwed."

"Red badge of courage," I told her. "Now eat your Coco Pops."

"Here, put this on it," said my sister, handing me a Band-Aid with a Teletubby on it. Clunk's fresh cut was on my biceps, but above it was an old scar, like a small triangle. I ran my fingers over it, but try as I might I couldn't remember when and how I got it. All I had was the fragment of my bad dream – and Hercules' voice saying, "Watch yourself, Fredboy!"

So I went and got our photo box from the trailer and brought it back out into the sunshine.

"What you doing?" sang Whitney, trying to see.

I showed her the old brown faded picture I'd dug out from the bottom of the pile. "That's your great-great-great-*great*-granddaddy, Hercules Smith," I told her.

It was a very old photo, faded and creased, of a man with a handlebar mustache and a lionskin draped over one shoulder like the Greek hero of the same name. I figure it'd been taken around 1850, when old Hercules had still been famous. When crowds had flocked to see him fight, and women had declared they loved him, and men had narrowed their eyes and wished they'd got his power. Our family knew old Hercules as well as we knew our living relatives. There wasn't many a night that went by without somebody telling a Hercules story, about his days in the funfair fight booths, about his time at the circus amazing the crowds, about the time they framed him for horse thieving and he disappeared, never to be seen again. According to my Great-Granny Kate who told fortunes, old Hercules was our guardian angel, watching over the Smiths.

"He looks like you!" Whitney said, snickering.

I pretended to cuff her across the ear for that. "Yeah, except for the mustache and the lionskin."

But she was right in that we both have the darkest of eyes, and the lucky Smith smile that's good for winning people over when doing deals. But that's where me and Hercules part company. His hair was long and black, making him a dead ringer for a WWE wrestler, while my hair gets cut, whether I want it or not, by Crystal and her demonic hair clippers. Last time she left me looking like a sea urchin, with spikes all over the place. And I sure as hell haven't got Hercules' build yet. At the moment I'm scrawny, but I've got big paws, so I reckon I'm going to grow into a Doberman and not a Jack Russell.

Whitney Jade stuck out her left foot and waggled her toes. "Mammy says I'm a mermaid because of Hercules."

I know it sounds weird, but she's right. Alongside the extrastrong muscles, Hercules had given some of us webbed toes on our left feet, but only the boys – we'd never seen it on a Smith girl before. Sweet Mercy, if Whitney Jade had inherited Hercules' strength as well as his toes, she'd shake the world.

I kicked my sneaker off and wiggled my foot at her. She looked at it sadly.

"It's not fair, us being mermaids, Fwed." She glanced enviously at her sisters. "We can't wear flip-flops."

"I see myself more as a dolphin," I told her. "And webbed toes are kushti; it shows we're Smiths, and we're special."

Crystal came over and leaned close to me.

"Are those boys at the bus stop anything to do with last night?" she said softly, so Joe couldn't hear.

Her husband Joe'd got a mirror propped up on the hood of his Range Rover and was shaving. He'd not spoken to me much during the morning so I think he was getting a bit fed up having me around all the time, bringing trouble his way. All Joe really wanted was what most travelers want: a piece of land to call his own, his family around him, and enough work to keep him busy.

"I don't think so," I said. "But I can't be sure."

Crystal stared at me with her dark eyes and moved baby Frisco from one hip to the other. "Does this mean we move again?" she said in a flat voice, untangling the baby's chubby mitts from her long black hair.

We couldn't go far because we were staying near her in-laws and there was plenty of work for Joe.

"It'll be the fifth time this month if we do," I said.

But Crystal wasn't listening to me anymore. She was squinting over my shoulder at something. I turned around and found a cop looming over me. Worse still, behind him were three police cars and four more gavvers.

₩₩

"Freedom Smith?" said the cop, looking at me like I was something nasty he'd found on his shoe.

"If it's about last night," I said quickly, standing up and moving away from the girls and their breakfast, "I told the policeman last night, the skinhead came to attack our camp and I saw him off, and –"

"Attempted murder is what we're here to talk about," interrupted the cop, and his face was like thunder. So Clunk was still alive, at least. But like I said, no one was ever going to believe I was an angel.

"We've taken a statement from a boy who witnessed the attack," said the cop, while the others watched me like hawks in case I decided to make a run for it. All except one, who was making funny faces at the little girls to cheer them up and reassure them, because they were still at their breakfast table, spoons halfway to their mouths, looking ready to cry. Jeez, even when you try to hate all cops, there's always one who does a human decent thing in the midst of the trouble.

"Did your witness tell you why they were hanging around our camp?" I said.

"They were just walking by," said the cop. "You picked a fight with them both. Then you chased one of them into the road, deliberately into the path of a bus."

I think I knew, even then, that nothing I could say would change that cop's mind about me, but I tried. "I swear to God I would never do anything like that. He ran away from me and didn't look where he was going!"

The cop sighed. "His friend was a witness, son."

My heart began thudding, and all the nightmares of my past, the ones where I was innocent but no one would believe me, flashed before my eyes.

"He had gas, he was going to burn our trailers down," I said, while in my head I began to calculate how many seconds it would take me to leap onto the table, onto the trailer roof, jump over onto the parking lot wall, and be off and running down the next street. My instincts figured I could be over the wall and in the street before the cop nearest to me had even gathered his wits together. But my brain said that I would be a fool to try, unless I wanted to be on the run forever, for something I didn't do.

"Proof?" said the cop.

"What?" I came back to the present.

"Do you have any proof?"

The fire had consumed the gas. The cop saw me hesitate and knew straightaway that I had no proof. That's when I gave up. I could've had a hundred witnesses and I swear he'd still have believed I'd tried to get Clunk run over.

But suddenly this didn't matter so much anymore, because a voice in my head was saying, *Something's wrong!* over and over.

"You're going to have to come down to the station with us to answer a few questions," the cop began, but all I heard next was, "blah, blah, blah..." because I'd stopped listening to his words. I'd even stopped thinking, because my human brain had shut down and my reptile brain had taken over. Something was wrong. *But I didn't know what.*

I felt my body go into a crouch and the hair on the back of my neck stand on end, and every atom in my body was saying, *Be alert....*

I stayed very still and I listened.

"Blah?" said the cop, looking annoyed.

But I didn't answer because now I was thinking like a reptile. And reptiles don't answer to cops. They don't answer to anyone.

Which is why my mammy always says that the old Hercules theory of using the reptile brain is dangerous. She says the reason we now have a human brain is that people soon began to realize that life is easier if you don't go around biting one another's heads off over small problems that can be solved in better ways. And my daddy would reply, "You're right, Relda, but put the lad in a tricky situation and it's probably going to be the reptile brain that gets him out of the mess. It's good at that. It doesn't think, it reacts. It survives at all costs."

And it seemed my daddy was right, because now my reptile senses had seen something I hadn't. Something dangerous that my human brain hadn't noticed.

"Blah blah?" said the cop again, making a signal to one of the others.

I think he thought I was about to make a run for it, me being guilty and all. His colleagues quickly surrounded me. Which was good, because when they moved I finally saw what had disturbed me. I must have had a partial sight of it as the cop was talking to me, but there were too many distractions for me to notice it straightaway.

It was a big black BMW.

It was parked on the corner some distance away, and the morning sun was reflecting blindingly off the chrome trim, making my eyes water as I tried to focus on it. The windows were tinted, but I thought I could just make out the looming silhouette of a man.

My blood ran cold. It was the spitting image of the dark car from my dream.

"Stay right where you are, son."

The policeman's voice brought me back to the present.

"What?" I said, probably sounding like an idiot. Then I realized that he was arresting me. He'd got the handcuffs out, and the others had closed in to give him support.

"Freedom, I want you to place your hands on the side of the trailer," he said. "Have you anything on you that could harm me or yourself?" I shook my head. "Keep your hands on the trailer. . . . I'm arresting you on suspicion of –" he began, but he didn't get any further. There was a tap on his shoulder and a policewoman said something quietly to him.

"Don't move a muscle, I'll be back," he said.

I stayed spread-eagled and watched from under my arm as he went over to the mysterious black car. I saw the window glide down a little, but the driver inside was still just a dark shape. There was a brief conversation and then the cop sauntered back over with a slightly bemused look on his face.

"Who's he?" I said when he came back to me.

"Never you mind," said the cop briskly. He looked uncomfortable now and the sweat was running down his face. I don't think all of it was due to the heat of the morning: Something was bugging him, and it wasn't me anymore. I was no longer the focus of his attention. He couldn't seem to take his eyes off the BMW.

"Well, well, well," he said eventually. "So you're *that* Smith, eh?"

I was a Smith, but I had no idea whether I was *that* Smith, so I said nothing. Which is a great step forward for me, because I usually open my mouth and put my foot right in it when I'm in a difficult situation like this.

The cop stared glassy-eyed at the car for a while longer, then back at me again. The gavver in the car had really rattled him.

"Jeez, my hands are going dead! Are you going to arrest me or shall we get the little girls lined up and let them limbo dance under my arms?" I said eventually.

The cop wiped the sweat from his face and looked at me sourly. "Well, Freedom Smith of no fixed abode, aren't you a lucky boy? Seems we're not arresting you." He poked me in the chest. "Seems you've got friends in high places." He pointed over toward the black BMW. "His Highness wants a word with you." Then he signaled to the other cops and they got back in their cars.

I waited until they'd disappeared around the corner, then I walked off in the opposite direction.

"Where you going?" yelled Crystal out the trailer window. "You're supposed to be talking to the man over there."

But I kept on walking.

"How long have you been married, Crys?" I shouted back over my shoulder.

She gave me a look like I'd gone crazy. "Ten years, God help me. Why?"

Because I had an image in my head of a black car outside our trailer, and me hiding my face in Crystal's wedding dress, hanging in my room ready for her big day.

I kept on down the street. The bad dream had haunted me for long enough, and I wanted answers. But I wasn't a scared kid anymore, and I'd talk to him when I was ready.

卌 ||

"*Hello, love, put me through to the boss, will ya?... Hi, Snow, it's Wren here...* crrrrrsssssht... *Sorry, reception's bad here, I'm in the multistory parking lot near the camp.... We've got a bit of a situation going on here. They let Smith go as per my instructions, next thing the boy's gone walkabout, completely ignored the instruction to come over and parley with me, and strutted off up the street....* crrrrrsssssht... *Oh yeah, I think he definitely remembers.... I know it's a different car, but it's still black with tinted windows, and it's triggered something in his subconscious.... No, I've not lost him! I've got myself this nice little spot where I can watch the camp and see what he's doing. He knows I'm here and he'll come to me when he's ready.... Whaddya mean it won't work? Snow, you have no faith...he's here in the parking lot now.... Yeah, he's right behind me at this moment, he thinks he's crept up on me...* crrrrrsssssht... *Signal's going!... Can't hear ya... OK, catch you later...."*

• • •

One of the neon lights was on its last legs. It was flashing on and off in the gloom.

"Hello, Freedom," he said even before he'd put his phone away and turned around.

He was good. He must've had the hearing of a bat, because I swear to God he couldn't have seen me.

I wiped the sweat from my eyes. I'd gone straight up the side of the parking garage, right to the fourth floor. There were plenty of footholds. Then I did a shimmy along a ledge and came in from behind him. He'd been there a good long while, unless he was a manic Tic Tac addict who could down whole packets of them in seconds. There were at least five of the little plastic cartons lying empty on the ground next to him. He also smoked small Café Crème cigars, because there were butts lying around and an empty tin, which probably explained the Tic Tacs.

Around us the parking lot was in semidarkness and stifling. Nothing stirred.

"And they say Gypsies leave their garbage lying around," I said, for something to say.

Seeing him for the first time had stunned me. He was a giant, for one thing. No wonder his shadow in the BMW had looked hunched over the steering wheel. No wonder he needed a big car. He was maybe six foot seven, the sort of height that means you have to duck to get through normal doorways. And he was wearing a cowboy hat that almost brushed the dingy concrete of the parking garage roof. He wasn't a rangy Clint Eastwood type, either; he looked like he could put out his hand and stop a tank. He stared at me for a couple of seconds like he was disappointed at what he saw.

"One, you were too noisy climbing up the side – if you're going to choose the direct route, do it from another angle, away from your target. . . ."

I backed against the parapet of the parking garage without taking my eyes off him. If he made one move toward me, I would be over the wall and down the side, as high as it was, before he could take another step.

"Two," he said, ticking the points off on his fingers, "I could've knocked you off your ledge the moment you stuck your head above the wall. If you're going to sneak up on someone, then don't put your own life at risk. And three –"

I didn't want to hear number three.

"What do you want with me, mister?" I butted in abruptly.

He had a cop's eyes, watchful and calculating. Most people meet another person's gaze for only a couple of seconds before they look away. Cops don't – they stare intently, that's why you can always spot them in a room. His eyes were bright blue in a leather face.

He grinned, showing a couple of gold teeth, and took out a thin cigar, then changed his mind. Instead he flicked open the lid of his Tic Tacs and emptied them into his mouth.

"I want you to work for us," he said, crunching the mints up.

I nearly laughed out loud at that. "You're the police, right?" I said.

He crunched some more. His eyes scrunched up but never left my face. "Something like that."

I wanted to say, *Get lost, leave me and my family alone, we're Gypsies, we don't deal with the police.* The police are nothing but trouble in our lives. The first thing I probably ever saw in my life was a cop evicting us from somewhere.

"The world's full of cops who can work for you," I said. "You don't need anyone else."

"We need a young boy, one who can fight. One who doesn't exist." He looked at me. "You're unique, Smith. We want you."

Well, he was the first person who ever had, and for the life of me I couldn't see why. So I didn't answer him, I had nothing to say, and the silence lengthened. His cell beep-beeped, but he ignored it. He hadn't moved an inch toward me, yet I still felt like he was backing me into a corner. I was leaning against the concrete strut, one leg dangling into the parking garage, the other dangling over a forty-foot drop, straight down. I could escape whenever I felt like it, but I was still trapped.

"Me work for you? Yeah, right. Like I need the police," I said, trying to pull my T-shirt away from my neck. It felt as though I was being strangled.

He considered this and then nodded. "You do need us. You're in big trouble, boy," he said. And my heart sank because I knew what was coming next, and I began to think that maybe this was a trap. "You chased that boy in front of a bus. Last I heard, he was on life support."

There they were again, the flash frames of Clunk getting hit, playing through my brain. I shook my head.

"It wasn't like that."

Wren shrugged. "There was a witness. The only thing stopping you getting arrested for attempted murder is me."

"Jeez, how many more times?" I said. "You lot just don't get it, do you? I was trying to push him out of the way."

He took out the cigar again. After a lot of patting at his navy blue bomber jacket, which must have been a police-issue garment for undercover cops because sure as hell it wasn't Dolce & Gabbana, he found himself a Zippo and lit his foul little cancer stick.

"Are you one hundred percent sure?" he said casually, out of the corner of his mouth, the smoke billowing around him.

I looked away, at a woman getting into a Fiat Punto farther down the row. Jeez, how could anyone be totally sure of anything? I've never intentionally hurt anyone in my entire life. Some people think I'm a demon, but they're people who don't know me and judge me by my ugly mug and my muscles. But the smell of gasoline had made me crazy, and when I'd chased Clunk I was working on reptile brain. Nothing's certain when that happens.

But I wasn't going to admit it to him. That was my own little nightmare for when I woke in the small hours with my mind on a loop. But by the look he gave me, I didn't need to tell him that.

"You're undisciplined, Smith," he said, chewing at the cigar. "You need us."

Like hell, I thought. I wanted out. I could throw myself off the parapet and drop like a stone until I caught hold of the ledge below. Or I could agree with him, and then walk away.

"I'm listening," I said.

He tapped the ash off his cigar and then squinted at me. "There's someone called Darcus Knight, ever heard of him?"

"Nope."

"He's heard of you," he said.

That made the hairs on the back of my neck stand on end. It seemed like every stranger knew me at the moment. Maybe if you wanted to become a pop star you'd be pleased with being recognized, but not me. I get into enough trouble without everyone knowing my name. I'm not in school, I have no fixed home, I haven't even got a birth certificate because I was born when we were traveling abroad and somehow the documents were never filled in properly for me. Like the man said, I don't exist and that's how I like it; yet suddenly everyone knows me.

"What does this bloke want with me, Wren?"

He looked at me. "Fighting."

"He wants me to be a boxer?" I said. "There's no chance of that."

Lots of traveler boys use boxing as a way to grab a bit of fame and fortune. Some of the Smith fighters had boxed and made a tidy living. I'd trained for a while, but no one wanted to fight me. Only one old coach would take me on, though he'd taught me loads. In the end I couldn't stand the rings, couldn't stand being closed in, or forced to fight just because a bell had been rung. And according to an old Smith story, nor could Hercules, because once he'd been forced to fight in a cage with a lion, and no one could get him near ropes or bars ever again.

Wren shook his head. "Darcus has gone far beyond boxing. This is something else."

"What?"

Wren spat out a strand of tobacco. "Ever heard whispers about the longest-running fight in the world?" he said.

I groaned. "Yeah, I have, it's an urban myth," I said. I was perching like a bird on the parapet now. "It's a tale fighters tell to get themselves excited."

"I wish to hell it was," he said. He leaned himself

against the hood of his BMW. "We've had rumors of it for years. CID have investigated; they've found nothing, just dead ends and false leads. It was written off as a myth, just like you say. But I work for Phoenix."

He stopped, like I was supposed to know about some police team named after a mythical bird. "It's our job to investigate the incredible and the unbelievable."

"Like?" I said as though I didn't believe him.

He thought for a moment, eyes narrowed. "Ever heard of Nanny chips?" I shook my head. "Well, a company called NanoTech is covertly making microchips to be implanted into kids – without them knowing. The idea being that the chips will act like a supernanny, monitored by satellite links and able to watch everything that a child does. The company will then convince parents it's a good way of keeping their kids safe from abduction and kidnapping. But that's not NanoTech's real reason."

A cold feeling swept over me. "That's science fiction. Anyway, a kid would know if they got implanted."

"Not when the microchip's small enough to be swallowed in a tablet or a vitamin pill, and locates itself in the stomach lining, completely undetected. It's not science fiction. But everybody thinks it is, so it gets passed to Phoenix, and we have to find out the truth. I'm working on the case now. We know the company wants to create an army of microchipped kids. We just don't know its next move, that's all." He smiled grimly. "But we will."

"So?" I said as though I wasn't impressed, even though my fists were bunching at the thought of someone microchipping me or any of my nieces.

"The truth is, the world's a much stranger place than you ever imagined, Freedom," Wren continued. "That's why Darcus's fight has run for so long. Everyone wrote it off as a myth. But I had a gut feeling it was real, so I took over the investigation. And we've tracked it down. It's worse than we ever thought."

"How much worse?" I'd said it before I could stop myself.

He didn't answer straightaway, just did a Clint Eastwood stare into the distance, chewing on the stub of the cigar. When he did start talking, his voice was low and deadly serious. He relit his cigar and leaned back on a concrete pillar.

"Darcus Knight's origins are a mystery. We know he's a filmmaker, a fight addict, an expert in brainwashing techniques and medical procedures. Sometime in the past, we don't know how far back, his family started staging illegal bare-knuckle fights, running their men into the ground like the old fairground entrepreneurs. But the thrill wore off and the fans wanted more."

"How can you have more than bare-knuckle?" I said.

And in a low angry voice he began to tell me. "They wanted Rome again, they wanted gladiators, they wanted blood and guts, men and boys fighting in pits for the pleasure of those rich enough to afford the ticket price of ten thousand pounds to see just one fight. And so what if boys and men got badly hurt? They were petty thieves running from the law, drug addicts trying to find money for a fix. Of course, some were professionals, hooked on violence, brutalized by fighting, and expecting only a short sharp life and nothing more. There's always fighters willing to risk all, lured by more money than they could ever imagine. But the fighting gets to their brains, and no one ever leaves and no one ever tells." Wren paused, and considered for a moment. "Given Darcus's skills, we suspect brainwashing or electronic implants."

He lit another cigar from the end of the first. The parking lot was deathly still now, the grimy neon light casting weird shadows that flickered and danced. I swallowed, but I couldn't think of anything to say. I'd thought he'd finished, but he'd saved the worst till last.

"The fight goes on, day and night," he continued, his voice harsh. "And ticket prices go through the roof for the star fighters, the ones who'll stop at nothing to win, who'll give the crowd the blood they crave. Sometimes the fight slows down, but it never stops. Never. It moves from secret location to secret location, and with each move its theme changes. This time it's a medieval bear pit, where men and boys on the run find sanctuary, and are paid fortunes to fight for their lives. It's been running so long that some boys have been born and brought up in it." He stopped again, tapping the ash from his cigar. He looked at me.

I swallowed again, but still couldn't find my voice. I didn't want to hear that there were people in this world who will breed boys like pit bull puppies.

But he only had to glance at my face to know that he'd got me now. He pointed his cigar at me. "They need boys just like you because it's the boys who command the big ticket prices. Men may have the strength, but only boys have the reactions and the speed. And they don't question it, because they are born into it, and some of them die in it, having never known anything else but the fight, day after day. And if nothing is done to stop it, more lost boys'll live their entire lives there."

I found my voice at last. "But why don't they escape, why don't they call someone?"

"No fighter has ever talked," said Wren. "None of the specially selected, high-paying guests have ever given the place away. Previous investigators have given up. But we've tracked it down."

I tried again. "So go and close it down, man!" I had another image in my head now, one to rival Clunk's run into the road. And it was of a small skinny kid staring blank-eyed at a brutal fight through an endless night.

"Every attempt by undercover officers to infiltrate the Bear Pit has failed," said Wren. "We've lost one man already. Gabby went in as a fighter and we've heard nothing from him since. We can't just barge in with a warrant, because we'd ruin everything we've done so far. We tried it once before, but Darcus denied everything and none of the fighters would talk. And afterward they just moved to another location and it took us years to find them again. We have to get someone inside, and they have to take part in a fight, get proof, and then testify." He looked at me with the eyes of an avenging angel, all fire and glory. And I knew what was coming next. I'd walked right into it.

"Darcus's fight fans pay the most money to see the young boys fight, lads your age. He's suspicious of older fighters and vets them hard. We think that's what happened to our man. But he knows the young kids aren't cops. You, Freedom Smith, you could get in without suspicion." He smiled grimly. "Let's face it, no one would think a Gypsy boy would be working for the police. And he's heard all about you."

My mouth had gone dry. "How?"

Wren seemed to be contemplating whether to tell me something. At last he said, "We've both been watching you for a long time, Freedom Smith. We know exactly what you can do; that's why we need you. You have something beyond strength and fighting ability."

And I thought, *Here we go again, this is all to do with old Hercules.*

"That's why Darcus wants you, too. As soon as he recognizes you he won't be able to resist." Wren was watching me closely. "You have inherited a dangerous gift, Freedom. Are you going to squander it?"

I didn't answer, just chewed the sore place on the inside of my cheek, trying to remind myself of how all this had started.

"Are you a freak fighting machine, or are you a hero?" he said quietly.

I shrugged. "I'm neither, I'm me, a Gypsy boy, I don't deal with the police."

He got his keys out of his pocket, tossed them in the air, and then beeped his car. The lights flashed and the locks clunked. He swung the door open. "OK, by tomorrow you'll be inside the police station being questioned. Maybe I'll see you in there." And he saluted me and got in the car.

"That's blackmail," I spat. "You gavvers, you're all the same."

He was still in the car but he hadn't shut the door yet. "Call me what you want," he said. "But let me tell you, I'm your savior."

Yeah, right. But through my mind went Clunk running into the road. And there was me, chasing him, without thinking, just reacting like a reptile. Is that what I wanted to be?

"Wait," I said.

||||| |||

"We're moving." Crystal was staring out the trailer window, chewing the end of her hair and watching for more trouble.

"I know a good place," I said, all innocence.

Nobody can pack like traveling people. It's probably in our blood, honed to perfection from the time the Dom left India. The way I've heard it told, the Dom were a tribe of dancers and musicians, but the other tribes didn't want them around. So they left and began looking for somewhere else to live. Maybe they thought they'd only be traveling for a few months at the most. Jeez, it took them a thousand years, and in that time Dom changed to Rom and then to Romany, and we've still not found a home yet. Too many people saying, "You can't park here," that's the problem.

So we packed and we moved and we did it with showmanship, to let everyone know we weren't trailer trash, pikeys, that we were proud of who we were.

"Where we going to pull onto next, Fwed?" said Whitney Jade, her eyes sparkling with excitement. She'd got hold of a can of Diet Coke and the caffeine had got to her. She could hardly sit still.

"We're going somewhere nice," I told her.

The little girls were in the backseat of our Mitsubishi Warrior, their faces as suntanned as little señoritas, their gold necklaces gleaming and their long dark hair brushed and up in ribbons. When Crystal was upset, or things had been going wrong for us, she always made sure the girls looked like they were daughters of millionaires. D&G Junior for the littlest, but Versace and Barbie boots for Whitney, who looked like a little rock star. She did the same with me, too, buying me Prada and Diesel tops and jeans so that I didn't go around with the same pair of Levi's hanging off me day after day. All I cared about were good sneakers, light and supple, preferably Nike, ones that would stick to roof tiles.

"Out in the country?" she asked.

"The country's boring." My daddy had once bought us a bit of land near the town, but we'd been stupid enough to get cheated by the landowner, a wealthy lord of the manor who owned a property company called Greenacres. We were fooled by the name and thought we'd bought acres of green land to live on, but he'd sold us green belt land, which meant it was against the law to live on it in our trailers. I'd gone off the countryside around here after that, although I was itching to meet that Greenacres boss, even if he was a lord of the manor, and have a quiet word or two with him.

"So where *are* we going, Fwed?" said Whitney Jade, jiggling about with glee. I swear to God, Diet Coke is worse than a drug for little kids.

"To the park," I said. What had Wren called it? "We're going to Penny Park."

Crystal swung the wheel. "We're here," she said.

She didn't have to tell me. My reptile senses had only just stopped tingling and off they went again.

● ● ●

It was like a clearing in the jungle, except the jungle around us was of the concrete variety. A small park, shaped like a penny and about the same size, the grass withered and crispy from lack of rain. It was surrounded by the backs of some factories, a pub, a café called Mrs. Bunn's, and an old building with a rusted Victorian sign on the gates that read CHEMICAL WORKS. Above it was a sleek modern sign, and this one said KNIGHT FILM STUDIOS.

This building was my target, and even on first glance it sent ice down my spine.

The mean staring windows were too small, and the walls were covered with blackened ivy. Where the roof began there were small bushes growing, but they were brown and dried out from the heat, so that it looked like the building had sprouted tufts of hair. It didn't look like a building that had been built out of anything as ordinary as brick; it looked like it had oozed up out of the ground and then solidified into a fortress.

The whole place looked well secured, despite being almost derelict. There were CCTV cameras on poles, and the gates enclosing the parking lot at the front were electronically controlled and looked strong enough to withstand a tank.

I wondered how the people in the studios were going to react when the camera turned our way and they saw us camped outside their gates. But it wasn't my problem for once. Wren had told me to come here.

"What do you think?" said Crystal.

"It's clear," I said as we pulled onto the grass. But that was for Crystal's benefit.

According to Wren, we were parking close to hell itself.

ᚑᚑᚑᚑ ||||

The red Spider had the top down; so did the silver BMW convertible next to it. In fact most of the cars in the parking lot were of the expensive kind, just as Wren had said. But that was what I'd expect from a film company. Didn't film producers always drive around in sports cars and have money spilling out of their pockets? Maybe Wren and the Phoenix cops were wrong, and it really was an honest company making programs for the cable channels.

Or maybe the five boys who were sitting in the cars had rich daddies, because I swear they were only perhaps a year older than me, seventeen at most.

Five pairs of shades turned toward me as I stared across at them. I waited for the jeers and the catcalls about us parking outside their place. Boys in a gang are the worst for shouting and making a mockery of people, but none did. They just stared for a moment or two, looked me up and down, and then carried on as though they weren't very impressed. Which was interesting, because it meant they didn't feel threatened. That's normally why kids react badly to those they don't know. They feel insecure, so they get their hackles up straightaway.

This group just got out of their cars, then came through a small side gate, skipping over the clumps of withered grass that had forced their way through the broken concrete of the parking lot. Five boys in track pants and tight T-shirts with the sleeves rolled right up to show their biceps. And the sight of them chilled my blood because Wren was right; these weren't just film crew or even actors, these were some of Darcus's fighters. Like jackals on the Serengeti, they looked all relaxed muscle, but underneath you could see the honed killing machines that would spring into action the moment an unwise antelope went by. Of course, the puffy lip on one of them and the massive purple bruise on another's upper arm were big clues as well.

It must have been home time because the park had got busy all of a sudden, and the jackals mingled in with workers leaving the other factories. A tramp sitting with his dog outside Mrs. Bunn's started begging for change and holding out his hat. A few of the workers dropped coins into it, but the jackals stepped over him. Then they went inside the café. Which was lucky, because it was my job to get the old milk churns from beside the trailers and fill them with drinking water.

When you live on the side of the road you don't get

luxuries like piped-in water, you have to fetch it yourself, and it becomes as precious as whiskey. So I had a good excuse for going over to Mrs. Bunn's. I grabbed one of the old churns in one hand and Whitney Jade's sticky mitt in the other, and went across.

"Now, what do you say to a knickerbocker glory, duckie?"

Inside the café the five jackals had installed themselves at the tiny tables, and were eating multicolored, many-layered ice cream concoctions in long tall glasses. They should've looked like they were enjoying themselves, but their faces were still blank, as though they were home alone, slumped in front of the TV, which made me twitchy because I hadn't a clue what was going on in their brains. The human brain likes expressions, it likes to know what might happen. With this bunch, I couldn't tell.

I needed to test them.

"Sorry?" I said to the old lady behind the counter, without taking my eyes off them.

"Would you like a knickerbocker glory, duckie?"

"Yes, please, ma'am," I said. I gave her my most charming smile, the one that doesn't frighten the horses too much.

"It's like heaven in here, Fwed," said Whitney Jade, standing on tippytoe and trying to see over the counter.

Mrs. Bunn smiled at us. "Oh, it is, it's paradise – and it's complete with my very own angel, darling!" And she winked as though there were a secret between us. Then she leaned closer to us and whispered, "It's Gabriel himself, you know, large as life!"

Her eyes were shining with happiness, as though she really did have an angel tucked away somewhere. But then I noticed what she was loading into the long glass. Sweet Mercy, it wasn't just ice cream – there was jelly and fruit and cream and all sorts of sprinkles going on.

"Now, isn't this a day of days!" she cried as she added a couple of chocolate flakes. "Wonderful Gypsy people right here on our doorstep!"

She was wearing a circle of flowers in her hair, like brides do, and a party dress with a bow, even though she was as old as my Great-Granny Kate. So, OK, maybe she was a little eccentric, but she was still happy we were here, which was a rarity.

"Wooden wagons, horses, the open road . . ." she said dreamily.

Who knows? If she could see angels, then maybe she did see horse-drawn vardos and campfires when she looked at our camp. All I saw out the window were our Ikea patio chairs and the little girls buzzing around the grass on their scooters and trikes.

She put my glass on the counter.

"Here," I said to Whitney, and gave her the knicker-bocker glory. "Now go and sit at that table with it."

She stomped off across the café and sat down near the jackals. I picked up a Tunnock's Caramel Wafer from the counter.

"Whitney!" She turned to me. I threw the wafer to her, overarm, like a hand grenade.

And five lean mean fighting machines were on their feet, too, and ready to pounce. They were fighters all right, with reflexes fine-tuned to counter any attack.

"Jeez, guys!" I said quickly, changing my body language to one of submission by sitting down, spreading my arms wide, and smiling. No one moved. A single long-handled spoon spun unheeded on a table and then fell to the floor with a tinkle. "It's cool!" I spread my hands again, palms upward, a gesture to show I had nothing to hide. "I was just passing my little niece her wafer, that's all!"

The jackals sat down and carried on with their knickerbocker glories. I glanced over at Mrs. Bunn, but she was humming "Amazing Grace" to herself and wiping down the counters, oblivious to what had just happened.

The bell on the door tinkled and someone came into the café behind me.

"My boys not being a bother, are they, Mrs. Bunn?" said a faint gasping voice. And a chill spread across the café.

I 卌 卌

My hackles rose. I'd never heard the voice before, but it grated across my nerves. Wren had been right. He'd said Darcus would come across as soon as he saw our trailers on the park.

"Ah, I see you've introduced one of our Gypsy visitors to your delightful ice cream, Mrs. Bunn!"

I turned around and froze.

He was old. Jeez, he was almost a mummy, his face like a skull with plastic-wrapped features over it, the hair gone except for a few wisps, his mouth shrunk back against his teeth in a permanent grin, like the Grim Reaper. His eyes were damp and yellow and they danced continually, even when he was staring, and he was staring at me now. And for all the heat of the day, he had over his bony shoulders a coat with a mangy gray fur lining. He must have had ice in his veins.

But the worst thing was, I recognized him. For a second I couldn't think how, then it came to me. I'd seen his nightmare face in that bad dream that was haunting me.

"Pleased to meet you, young man," he said, and held out a cold claw to me. I ignored it. He acknowledged the insult with a smile. It was almost a snarl, his lips were so drawn back. "I'm Darcus Knight. I own the old chemical works over there. Well, in fact it's a small film company now." He pointed toward the studios.

I pretended to give it a look and then shrugged. I was here to find out all I could about Darcus Knight and talk my way inside his company, but that didn't mean I had to be polite. Jeez, my heart had only just stopped thumping after the fright of seeing his skull-like face.

"What's that to me, mister?" I said. "I suppose you're going to tell me next that you want us to move or you're going to tell the police. Right?" I spread my arms wide. "But you can go and tell the police what you want. I don't care about them or anyone else, is that clear?" I gave him a sideways look. "We've just had a bit of a run-in with the police, anyway," I said. "But I tell you one thing – we ain't moving again."

Darcus was listening to me with his head to one side and his arms folded, as though he found me amusing.

"You're not a great fan of the police, then, I take it?" he said, raising an eyebrow.

"No, mister," I said. "And the feeling's mutual; they hate me, too." I swear it was hard to know whether I was playing it up for Darcus's benefit, or whether I was speaking the truth.

He looked me over, tapping his yellow teeth with a

mottled fingernail. He ought to have been dead, judging by the state of his skin. He looked like he was decaying.

"What made you and your family stop in this particular spot, boy?" He gave me a hard calculating look that chilled me to the bone.

"Go blame the council," I said with a sneer. "It's the last park in the whole town that's not got boulders at the gates or heaps of dirt around it to stop us getting the trailers in."

"Hmm," he mused, and nodded to himself. If he'd been suspicious that a Gypsy boy he'd once watched had turned up out of the blue, he wasn't anymore. That's if he'd recognized me. Wren said he would, but I wasn't so sure. It'd been a long time.

He swaggered over to the counter. "A coffee, please, Mrs. Bunn," he said, and lifted a rosebud from the vase on the counter, snapped the stem, and fitted it into his lapel. It looked like a scarlet bullet hole over his heart.

"One coffee coming right up, Mr. Knight," trilled the old lady. She glanced over at me while she filled his cup. "Mr. Knight makes films, you know! Sports films, to keep us in top shape!"

Darcus modestly bowed his head.

"He's a pillar of the community," Mrs. Bunn continued, her eyes dreamy. "He works with all the local schools, don't you, Mr. Knight? His programs teach the joys of exercise. Health and fitness are his top priorities for young people."

Yeah, right, I thought, but not how Mrs. Bunn was imagining.

Whitney Jade tugged at my hand urgently.

"I want to go back to Mammy," she said in a quiet voice. She was looking at Darcus from under her eyelashes. He'd freaked her out. She wasn't the only one.

"No, stay here," I whispered.

Whitney's lip turned down, and she stamped her little Barbie boot at me. "I want Mammy." She'd already devoured half of the knickerbocker glory and she'd destroyed her clothes in the process.

"You don't leave without me, there's a road to cross. Remember the survival skills I taught you?"

"Duh!"

I pointed to one of the posters in the café window. "See that Johnny Sparrow? He went wandering off and hasn't come back yet."

"Yes, it's a dangerous world for the unwary!" I looked up to find Darcus staring down at me again and stirring his coffee.

"Do you fight, Gypsy boy?" he wheezed.

"I do, mister." I put a cynical smile on my face. Wren would have been proud of my acting. "Last bloke that tried something with me is in intensive care."

Darcus inclined his head. "I could use a fighter," he said. "And I pay well."

I narrowed my eyes at him, secretly enjoying sneering

at him. "I'm a Gypsy boy, mister. I don't work for people. Especially I don't work for gorjers."

"These boys work for me," he said, ignoring me. He gave a small smile, one that didn't reach anywhere near his yellow eyes. "They earn more money than you could ever dream about."

He nodded toward the jackals.

They were sitting still and watching him. They looked almost normal until you studied their body language carefully. One was rocking backward and forward slightly; another was rubbing his leg over and over again as though trying to rub away an ache or something.

"They're magnificent," said Darcus, a vulture's smile on his face as he surveyed them. "And the rewards of, um, helping me with my films are magnificent, too. Did you see their cars?"

Magnificent the jackals might have been, but they sure as hell weren't fully human. I couldn't imagine them going to the movies, or rolling around laughing at something someone said.

"A bit flashy, if you ask me," I said, like I wasn't impressed. "And you can tell them from me, if they start anything with my family over there" – I nodded to where Crystal was hanging out the washing on the line Joe had strung up for her – "they'll be in intensive care, too."

He glanced out the window at Crystal, and his eyes began to dance. He put up a hand to hide the smile that came to his lips.

"Your sister?" he said.

But he didn't need to ask. He'd recognized her all right. I might've changed in the years since he last spied me, but Crystal hadn't. She'd always been beautiful; no one forgot her. He'd got his positive ID. He knew who I was, just as Wren had said. And he wouldn't let me get away this time.

"Well, boy, I hope you have the fighting ability to go with that fighting talk."

"I have," I said.

"Your family must be glad to have you around." He smiled.

I gave a hollow laugh. It was a pretty good one. "No one's glad to have me around, mister. I'm nothing but trouble. But I'll be gone soon." I gave a bitter look over to the camp. "Then they'll all be glad."

"That's a —!" began Whitney Jade, who'd been listening and looking at Darcus with her lower lip trembling. I knew she was about to say that it was a lie, that my family did love me, and that I wasn't going to leave them, so I quickly shoved a spoonful of jelly and ice cream in her maw. I didn't want Darcus to know we were close-knit. I wanted him to think I had no one and nothing. "Shut up, Whitney, and don't speak with your mouth full!" I warned.

I glanced over at Darcus, to see if he'd noticed, and I swear just that quick peek at his dreadful face triggered something in my brain. The bad dream flooded back again. But now it had moved on from the black car. There was just me crouching on the side of a road, Crystal trying to shield me, someone shoving her aside and then jabbing me in the arm with something sharp, and Darcus's face looming toward me, etched by the moonlight. And all the time old Hercules' voice is in the back of my head, saying, *Stay still, this is not the time to fight, you can't win now. All in good time.*

I shook my head and blinked. Maybe I'd cried out or something, because when I glanced at Darcus again, he was watching me with his head to one side. So I put a scowl on my face.

"You leave us alone, we'll leave you alone," I said. I nodded toward the jackals. "If those are your best fighters, I'd hate to see your worst."

But the threats and insults just made Darcus smile more, if you could call that death grin of his a smile.

"It's been a pleasure to meet you, Freedom," he said, putting his coffee cup down. "Come and see me tomorrow, and we'll talk about fighting and money." He held out his corpselike hand again. I ignored it again.

"Jeez, mister, how many more times? I don't deal with gorjers. I don't deal with anyone," I said, grabbing Whitney Jade's hand and starting to leave. But then I stopped and whipped around on him as though I'd just realized something. "So how did you know my name?" I said accusingly. I was standing too close to him now, invading his space, threatening him now.

Out of the corner of my eye I saw one of the jackals rise to his feet, slowly but with every muscle tense, like a spring ready to unleash. Darcus gave a small twitch of his hand, barely perceptible, but the jackal froze. Dear God, how well trained were these boys?

"I saw you walking across to the café just now," said Darcus, hardly missing a beat. "And I thought, there walks a fighter if ever I've seen one!" He pointed over to Joe, who had got the ponies out on the grass and was watering and feeding them. "And I heard him call out to you."

Liar, I thought. Everyone calls me Fred, except Whitney, who calls me Fwed.

Darcus grinned his grim-reaper grin. "Do you know, I think we're going to get on like a house on fire, me and you, Freedom," he whispered. "I look forward to seeing you tomorrow!"

I gave a short laugh. "No chance, mister."

And with that we went our separate ways. He led his boys back to the studios. They all trailed after him without a murmur, walking along behind him without moving their arms, as though they were carrying heavy bags in each hand. I went around to the back of Mrs. Bunn's with Whitney and we got our water.

I had made first contact, just like Wren had asked, but doing it my own way. Don't get me wrong, I wasn't working for Phoenix. I was working to redeem myself for Clunk's injuries.

"He was a very bad man, wasn't he, Fwed?" said Whitney, when she was sure Darcus was far away.

"He was indeed," I replied. "A bad man, but good for my redemption."

"What's that mean?" said Whitney.

"When you do something bad, like when I chased Clunk into the road, even if you know you never meant to do harm, then you have to pay something back. You have to show everyone else you're not a bad boy. It's called redemption."

"And then Clunk won't die, and the cops'll leave you alone?"

I picked up the full churn. "That's what I'm hoping. Now let's get this water back home."

◆ ◆ ◆

One of Wren's undercover men had gone into Darcus's fight and had never come back.

Dear Lord, what was I getting myself into?

◆ ◆ ◆

"Hello, love ... put me through to Snow, will ya? ... Hi, Snow, yeah, Freedom's off and running, and he's already not doing as he's told.... Yes, I know you warned me, but he'll come through. It's the Hercules gene – there's no one around who can beat him, so he always gets his own way. But this is our best chance to stop Darcus. And anyone else who wants to use Freedom. Now that every

criminal scientist in the world is secretly gene splicing, the boy could be lethal in the wrong hands.... Yes, I've briefed him on how to contact us in an emergency.... I'll catch you later, I've got another call coming through.... Yo, hello... Lauren! Hi, nice to hear from you, babe.... Yeah, sure, let's get together again.... Can't tonight, though, we've got a big case up on the board and running..."

‖ ⳾⳾⳾⳾ ⳾⳾⳾⳾

"Crystal, do you remember me saying I used to see a black car watching me?" I said as we danced. "And I'd run into your trailer and hide?"

As night fell a whole bank of writhing black clouds had swept in over the park and covered the sky. There was thunder coming in, I could feel it, like a giant hand pushing down on us and squeezing the air out of our lungs. So we were outside, dancing and playing our music.

Everything would have been OK except I couldn't stop looking at the studios, and I couldn't stop thinking about my bad dream. And how it was turning out to be a terrible memory, not a dream at all.

Crystal stopped jiving. She raised one of her perfect film-star eyebrows.

"Yeah, I remember. You'd have this dream that it parked outside the trailers at night, just to spy on you. You'd got a thing about strangers watching you." She smiled and ruffled my hair, like I was a kid again. "You were always making up stories. Once you hurt your arm and you said that a bad man had done it."

I glanced over at the studios again. "I reckon those things might be real. Did you ever see anything, Crys?"

She rolled her eyes heavenward. "No. Because it was a dream, that's all."

"You saw nothing?" I persisted. "You never noticed anything weird?"

I thought she was going to tell me to leave it, but she didn't. She fiddled with one of the gold hoops swinging from her ears.

"Once I went outside to go for a pee and I heard something, and for some reason I thought it was you running away! But when I got back in, I looked at the clock – two hours had gone by." She looked up at me and laughed. "Two hours for a pee!"

My mind started to rewind like a videotape, back to the past. And for a second I saw Crystal huddled by the side of the road with me, being my guardian. But then, as usual, the images faded – it was as though someone had pressed STOP and then fast-forwarded straight back to the present.

I put my hand up to feel the scar, but Crystal grabbed it. "That's all in the past, so forget about it." She smiled at me. "Put those webbed toes to some use, and let's jive. You always say it's good fight practice."

She was right. Have you ever seen really hot dancers jiving? Their feet hardly touch the floor, it's all bouncing and push-and-pull, using their partner's strength to get the momentum going, so they can throw 'em over their head or slide 'em across the floor without any sweat. I fight like that, I bounce off the walls, the floors, other people, anything, I steal their strength and I never stop moving on my toes, so I'm never where people think I'm going to be.

"This is the life, isn't it?" said Crystal, turning the music up louder. "I like this place!"

She was right, it should have been a great place to camp, and in an ideal world it would have been. If only there wasn't always someone coming around to say, "You can't park here," or someone who wanted to burn us out of our homes.

I looked at Whitney Jade and the little girls and I thought, *Jeez, what will it be like when they grow up? Will it be worse or better?* So I jived with Crystal and practiced fight moves in my head, so that I'd be ready if we were attacked again. The security cameras from the studios turned and pointed our way. And the passersby cutting through the park on their way home, or walking their dogs on the grass, stared at us and smiled, or hurried past as though they were scared.

When I'd had enough I stepped out of Crystal's way. "That's it for me," I said. "Joe! Come and dance with your woman."

Crystal was wrong about the black car being in the past.

I needed to talk to Wren.

● ● ●

The beggar with the dog was still sitting outside Mrs. Bunn's. The dog had a neckerchief tied around its neck, and its tongue was lolling out as it panted in the heat. The man had put a dirty, greasy old cap out front, but there were only a few pennies in it. I stroked the dog's ears for a minute, and it wagged its tail and panted happily at me. It was better at disguise than its master. Since when do dossers, tramps, and beggars have clean fingernails?

"I need to speak to Wren urgently," I said. Then I put a coin in his hat and walked off.

||| ++++ ++++

lounged on the corner. After a while the black car slid silently up. The passenger door clicked open and I got in.

"I'm not wild about this," said Wren, pulling away at speed. "So it better be important."

The inside of the car was sleek and filled with gadgets and buttons. He even had a small video screen below the dashboard.

In a couple of minutes Wren'd got us on the empty outer-ring road and we were eating up the miles.

"So what's bugging you?" he said.

"Who was in the black car ten years ago?" I said. There was enough reflected light for me to see his eyes. He knew what I was talking about.

"My boss, Snow."

"Why?" I said.

Wren spoke into empty air. "Connect me to Snow." The video screen flickered.

"Snow here," said a black silhouette. Either Snow was camera-shy or the lighting was bad. The voice had a metallic quality, too, as though it had been put through a mixer to disguise it.

"I've got Freedom Smith here, boss. He wants to know about the black car that followed him around when he was a kid."

"Hello, Freedom," said Snow.

I said nothing. He didn't seem bothered.

"We were guarding you," he continued. "And you were certainly difficult to guard!" He laughed. "You kept shooting out of that trailer in the middle of the night and catching us. It was a good thing our Phoenix boffins had developed a short-term memory wipe or we'd have been scuppered." He paused. "A memory wipe that obviously didn't work as well as we thought, or we wouldn't be having this conversation. But then again, you are rather a special case."

I took a deep breath. "Why did you chase me one night and stick a needle in my arm?"

"We didn't," said Snow immediately. "Surveillance and protection only. That was our brief."

It seemed like my bad dream had jumbled all the memories together. Phoenix might have shadowed me, but someone else had scarred my arm. I was betting that that someone was Darcus.

I pulled up my sleeve and showed Wren. He nodded. "He's got a small triangular scar, boss. Looks like someone took a tissue sample and blood."

"It's nothing to do with us," said Snow. "We did lose

you once, though. We found you huddled by the side of the road half a mile away. Your sister had gone out looking for you. We had to mindwipe you both."

No, the mindwipe hadn't worked. My head was still full of half-memories that my brain kept trying to sort out. It had worked on Crystal, though – she just thought she'd spent two hours having a pee.

I gave a sarcastic laugh. "The cops guarding a Gypsy boy? Why?"

Wren was tearing down the main road through town now. The engine ran like silk, and the only noise I could hear was the faint creaking of the leather seats.

"We were protecting you from people who wanted your, um, skills. Imagine if someone could copy your strength and fighting skills and then give them to a thousand other boys, and make themselves an unbeatable army of superstrong fighters."

"Might be OK," I said.

"Not if that person is Darcus Knight," said Snow. "That's why we want you to help us stop him before he gets you."

"I never heard tell of Uncle Shady or Granddaddy Bartley getting their own private bodyguards. And they had fighting skills."

"They weren't you, Freedom," said Snow.

"So what's different about me?"

The figure on the screen was still for a moment. Wren gunned the BMW around a traffic island. "The difference is that you have the Hercules gene," Snow said eventually. "Call over." And the screen went blank.

There was silence in the car.

"Are you going to tell me what the Hercules gene is?" I said to Wren.

We'd come full circle and we were approaching the side road to Penny Park again.

Wren stepped on the brakes. "Nope. It could jeopardize the mission. You have to know as little as possible, so there's no chance of you giving anything away."

"But –"

"Out you get, Freedom."

My door clicked open. I got out, then ducked my head back in. "How come we've just driven around town and we didn't hit a single red light? That's not possible."

Two small lines appeared at the side of Wren's mouth. It might've meant he was smiling. "Phoenix perks," he said, and drove away.

I watched the BMW disappear, then looked at my watch. It was the unholy hour. Time for me to get my fix.

◆ ◆ ◆

"Snow? Are we doing the right thing not telling him everything? He doesn't know the half of it where Darcus's fight is concerned. Thank God he doesn't know about Hercules' connection to it. The Smith family worship the memory of the old fighter! . . . What? Yeah, get the kettle on, I'm coming back to HQ."

|||| ⊬⊬⊬ ⊬⊬⊬

Adrenaline and chili are my two addictions.

I balanced on the highest point of Mrs. Bunn's roof, crouching like a peasant and eating Thai green curry with noodles, hot enough to make my eyebrows sweat. There was no moon because of the storm clouds, but they were so low that they were bouncing back the lights from the city center, giving the sky a dull orange glow. On the horizon in every direction, lightning flickered and flared.

I had a clear view from up here of the park, the pub, and the surrounding buildings: the whole of Phoenix's surveillance sector. The pub was closed and the customers long gone. The studios looked quiet, but there were cars in the parking lot, and dim lights showing through some of the windows. Right on the cusp of my hearing I could just make out a distant roaring coming from there. It sounded like lions, a long way away.

I changed my position and looked down into the café yard. The yard was spick-and-span and full of tubs of flowers and a sun lounger. But on the flat shed roof there was a bundle of blankets or a sleeping bag and a backpack. My first thought was that a beggar was sleeping up there during the mild summer nights. But I didn't have time to speculate much more. A dainty foot in a Doc Marten came out of nowhere and power-kicked me in the stomach.

I had just enough time to see the girl's face, tinted orange from the storm clouds above and growling like a bear. Then a small fist that looked like it was made of bird bones came out of nowhere and punched me right on the chin. I went over backward, did a dramatic rolling slide down the roof, and cartwheeled off the gutter before catching hold of a drainpipe.

Miss Bird Bones must have thought she'd kicked me right off the edge, because I heard her gasp, "Omigod!" in that horrified all-in-one way that gorjer girls do, even when they've only broken a nail. Which meant she'd be temporarily stunned at what she'd just achieved with her medium-strength kick and a frankly substandard punch.

I have a chin as hard as Desperate Dan's, so I knew she'd be sitting there sucking her knuckles. Which would give me just enough time to swing myself back up all in the same move, scuttle like a high-speed crab back up the slippery, moss-covered tiles, and have the girl sprawled on the roof ridge and in an armlock before she even realized what was happening.

So that's exactly what I did.

"Ow! Get off, you oaf!"

Oaf! What sort of girl calls someone an oaf?

"Let me guess, you've studied tae kwon do," I said into her ear. Jeez, even her arms felt like they had bird bones. She should've had my mammy feeding her as a baby; Smith children grow up feeling like they're made of lead. "I recognize the style of the punch, but I bet you've never punched anything more than a practice pad."

Instead of answering me, she got her chin clear of the roof tiles. "You better know what you're doing," she gasped. "Or you're going to be heading off the roof again very quickly."

"Brave talk," I mocked. "I'd applaud your bluffing but I don't want to let go of you."

I felt her try every move in the book for getting out of the armlock, but she didn't succeed. After that the fight seemed to go out of her, but I still didn't let go. She smelled of something that reminded me of my childhood, something comforting, but I couldn't think what it was.

Cinnamon?

"Please!" she said, in a small muffled voice now. A wind had sprung up from nowhere and was blowing her fair hair across her face, so I couldn't see who I'd armlocked. "You don't understand! I'm so sorry, I was frightened, you came out of nowhere!" she whispered, and then she did something awful. She burst into tears.

I should know about tears – I have seven sisters and loads of nieces – but I never learn.

For the second time in two days I relaxed an armlock on somebody who had just attacked me. Maybe those people who think I'm a demon should witness all the times I've loosened my grip because my opponent has given me a sob story, and a split second later I'm on the receiving end of a punch. It happened again this time. One minute she was lying there sobbing, fit to break her heart, and the next she'd turned around like a hellcat, in a flurry of cutoff denims, Docs, and a sloppy-joe sweater that was hanging off her shoulders and trailing over her bird-boned hands. And then she kicked me straight back down the roof again.

"I hope you really are a bird and you can fly," I gasped as I headed toward the gutter again. "Because you're coming with me," and I grabbed her thin ankle.

There was a distant rumble of thunder, like a drumroll, and we slid down to oblivion together.

|||| |||| ||||

If I was hoping she would scream in fear, then I was disappointed. She never made a squeak, even though I let her slide nearly all the way over before I braked and hoisted us both up.

Something clinked in her pocket. There was the smell again, but I couldn't make it out. It reminded me of winter.

"Truce," she said when we reached the safety of the chimney stack. She rested herself against it, with her legs drawn up and her arms hugging her knees, until she'd caught her breath. Then she fumbled in the pocket of her cutoff jeans, got out a small tin, and lit a roll-up.

"Want one?" she said.

"No, thanks, love, I don't smoke," I said quickly. It's always been a bit of an embarrassment to me, and something I consider a serious flaw in my character, that I have none of the common vices. In another life I was probably a saint or something.

She sat there puffing away, illuminated by the lights around the park and the ominous orange glow of the massed thunderclouds above us. She looked chastened, but I kept well away. Her idea of a truce was probably to wait until I was smiling and then kick me in the teeth.

Nothing like that happened, however. She just stared at me angrily for a while, threw the butt end of the roll-up away, and then spat out, "What do you know about my brother?"

Her face said, *I'm as hard as nails, I'm not scared.*

Which was interesting because she had her arms wrapped around herself like she was giving herself a bear hug, and her thumbs, which you could just see beneath her trailing sleeves, were tucked into the palms of her clenched hands for comfort.

I perched myself like a bird on the roof ridge, where I could watch out for any move she might make. "I don't even know who your brother is, love."

She squinted at me. "Don't call me 'love,'" she said icily. "I know something's going on here."

"Yeah, you tried to kick me off a roof." Medicine, that's what she smelled like. Herbal medicine.

"Too right!" Her eyes were blazing like lasers. "Care to tell me what you were doing up here?"

"Care to tell me what *you* were doing up here?"

She didn't answer straightaway, just started fiddling with her sweater, which had slipped off one of her shoulders. She pulled it back up and then bear-hugged herself again. See, that was the sort of thing that vexed me about her. One part of me was thinking she was nothing but trouble, while the other half of me was catching its breath and unable to take its eyes off her.

"I'm looking for my brother," she said at last. She had one of those voices that went with private schools and vacations abroad. "This is the last place he was seen before he disappeared off the face of the earth."

She sniffed tearfully and wiped her nose with her trailing sleeve. I had to suppose that these were genuine tears for her brother. She would hardly be up on a roof, risking her life, if she didn't care much for the guy. I tried to see if there was any difference between these tears and the earlier mock ones, but I couldn't spot anything, and this is from someone who prides himself on noticing every little twitch of body language and every nuance of voice – when fighting a man. The thing is, I have a problem with girls; I just can't get the hang of them.

"Is your brother Johnny Sparrow?" I said as some light began to dawn, and a shadow moved, letting one of the park lights etch her face in silver. I could see the similarities between the boy on the poster with his pointy-chinned face, like a Japanese cartoon character, and this girl, with her pointy face, short hair, and frankly pointy ears as well. The whole effect was of a bad-tempered elf.

"See! You *do* know something," she said accusingly.

"I read the poster," I told her. "They're everywhere."

She gave a disappointed sigh and then sat hugging

her knees and looking out across the rooftops in a hopeless way. "I thought maybe I'd found a lead," she said, sounding tired to death. Then she reached into her pocket again and took out the bottle that had clinked earlier, uncorked it, and took a swig. She held it out to me. "Want some?"

Jeez, what now, I thought. First the roll-ups, then booze. I was going to have to say no again, but it did my credibility no good at all. "I don't drink," I said.

"It's Buttercup cough syrup," she said. That was the smell! "My mum gave it to me when I was little. It reminds me of her." She held it out again, but I shook my head. Then I froze.

Across the park the studio door opened and voices echoed.

"Down!" I hissed, throwing myself flat on the slates and pulling her after me. Then I shuffled up to the roof ridge and risked a look over. Two of the jackals had left the studios through a side door and were having a serious car discussion over the hood of one of the convertibles. The studio door was still ajar.

"What the hell was that about?" said the girl angrily. But she hadn't got my attention anymore. OK, I was intrigued by this cough-syrup drinker who haunted the rooftops. But that studio door had just made my future plans a whole lot easier.

"Got to go," I said. I slid down the roof, then leaped down onto the flat extension behind the café. A feral tabby hissed and scuttled away. I leaned out and took a peek at the parking lot. The two jackals still had their heads under the car hood, while the side door creaked in the breeze. Between them and me there was a medium-to-difficult run across the roofs of two abandoned factories.

"Boy! Wait."

I glanced back at the girl. She was watching me intently, her lips moving slightly as though she was talking to herself. Then she began to slide down after me.

"Look, love, I've got to go someplace," I told her again. "On my own."

"Don't call me 'love,'" she said, still sliding. "I've just been talking to my mum, actually."

I was testing the drainpipe running up the factory wall to the roof, prior to disappearing up it like an Indian magician up a rope, but that stopped me. For a second I thought she'd got a Bluetooth headset on and she'd called an irate parent for backup against a bad boy like me. But there was nothing behind her pointy ears.

"Run that by me again?" I said.

She jumped down onto the extension and fixed me with a steady gaze. "My mum died when I was little, but I always ask her what she thinks if I've got a hard decision to make. I make better choices that way."

So, let's add talking to dead people to the cough syrup and the roll-ups. I should have laughed at her, but I'd heard all this sort of stuff before from Great-Granny Kate, who swore that her dead husband used to blow in her ear to tell her to change channels when he got bored of a TV show.

"Does she answer?" I said.

She gave me a pixie smile. "No, I just suddenly know what choice I should make. This time I asked her if I should trust you."

"And?" I said.

"She said yes."

"A mammy other than my own thinking I'm trustworthy? That's a first, love."

"Java," she said. "My name's Java."

Java Sparrow? Now what sort of name was that, for heaven's sake?

She stared at me steadily, her eyes aglow, like a cat. "And my mum is never wrong."

Yes, well, I suppose you can be infallible when you're dead and someone's putting words in your mouth.

I didn't wait to hear any more. I got my hands around the drainpipe and shimmied up it, fast. If the truth be told, she was worrying me and I didn't know why. Maybe it was because I considered the rooftops to be my own kingdom, the one place where I couldn't put my foot in it or get into trouble with anyone. She'd kicked herself into my world, trailing the scent of cough mixture and Golden Virginia smoke, and I was dazed and confused. A quick dangerous run and then a bit of burglary should sort me out.

The roof of the first factory was a minefield of glassless skylights, broken roof tiles, and razor-sharp trip wires. In daylight I could have run across at speed. In the dark, it was tricky.

"Oh wow, this is amazing," said Java, climbing deftly onto the roof beside me.

Dear Lord, she was unstoppable. "Go back," I said. "Unless you want to take a swift trip to the ground floor via a hole in the roof."

"Maybe Johnny came up here," she said, ignoring me and taking a few unwise steps across the corroded old roof. "Maybe there are clues."

I grasped her arm and made her sit down on a ventilation turret. "Never walk on a roof without testing each step," I said. "Now, just tell me what's going on." I glanced at the studio parking lot. "And make it quick."

"There was a row at home," she began. "Johnny argued with Dad. Dad's got this girlfriend that we don't like. So Johnny just quit school and ran away. To begin with he phoned me and told me he was living rough but he'd made friends."

It sounded like a recipe for disaster to me. A rich boy suddenly trying to survive on the streets. He'd be the target of any number of lowlifes.

"I know what you're thinking," she said. "That Johnny was a spoiled kid who couldn't look after himself?"

I nodded. There was no use lying.

She stared bleakly out over the rooftops for a moment

and began swapping the little silver rings from the fingers of her left hand to the fingers of her right. "You have no idea," she said. "We were brought up by nannies, and I don't know how my dad managed to do it, but they were all evil witch-trolls. Then we both went to boarding school at seven years old, to be out of his way. At eight I knew my way around most of the airports in Europe and how to catch a flight on my own. We've spent Christmases and birthdays alone with just staff for company. We might've had everything, but we learned early on not to rely on anyone but ourselves."

All the rings had swapped hands now, so she started to put them back.

"My mum made sure we were taught martial arts, rock climbing, orienteering ... anything that'd help us survive. She knows Dad isn't looking after us very well. That's why I'm worried about Johnny. He's the Junior All England Karate Champion. He isn't a pushover."

All the karate in the world wouldn't save him from a hardened thug with a baseball bat or a brick in a sock, I thought.

"Last time I heard from him he phoned to say he was sleeping on the shed behind a café called Mrs. Bunn's. He said he'd met someone who'd got a job for him, but he wouldn't tell me what it was. Then I never heard from him again. The police investigated but couldn't find anything. So I left it until Dad went to our villa in Gozo for the summer, and then I found the café and came here. I figure that if I wait here long enough, whatever happened to him will happen to me." She paused. "But I'll be ready for it."

I couldn't believe I was hearing this correctly. Dear Lord, my mammy would go mad if she knew a young girl was out all night on her own. Thunder was rumbling over the rooftops almost continuously now, and the lightning was getting closer.

"I'm sorry for your troubles," I said, getting up and moving gingerly across the treacherous roof. "But I have enough of my own. Why don't you go home and let the police sort it out?"

"I can't," she said, starting to follow in my footsteps.

"Why?"

"I did something in case I changed my mind when the going got tough."

She didn't elaborate, but she'd probably written her dad a nasty note, or been rude to the chauffeur.

"OK, good luck with your quest," I said. "Now go back to the café roof. Don't come any farther."

She nodded. I began moving across the roof, picking my footsteps with care, feeling for the rotten tiles before trusting them with my weight, feeling for the invisible wires that were waiting to trip me. I skirted a patch of black where the roof had collapsed, and reached the other side. Something touched me on the shoulder.

"What the –?"

"I've got money for a reward," said Java, appearing at

my side. "If you help me find my brother, you'll be rich."
She saw the look of horror on my face. "I walked in your
footsteps," she explained crossly.

"Jeez, what are you? A reincarnated cat burglar?" I
growled. Then, "You want me to be a *bounty hunter?*"

"Yes."

We were facing each other on the rickety roof, the
lightning near enough to reflect in our eyes.

"No," I said. "Now go back!"

She gave me a pixie smile. "I can't remember the way."

I looked across at the next factory roof. Between the
two was a chasm three floors deep with a Dumpster full
of scrap iron at the bottom. Not the softest of landings
if I missed my footing. The good thing was, there was no
way she could follow me across there. I eyed the distance
to the next roof. It would be a stretch even for me, and a
leap of faith, because ideally I'd practice a jump this
wide lower down, where it didn't matter if I fell. But I'd
been roof-jumping for years, and instinct told me I could
make it.

"You're not going to jump across there, are you?" she
said, watching me with her laser gaze. "It's too far."

"Feel the fear and do it, that's my motto." There was a
fire escape ladder leading off our roof and down to the
ground. I took ahold of it and gave it a good shake. It
was solid enough to take Java's bird weight.

"Is that the place you're going to?" she said, ignoring
the ladder and nodding over toward the studios. She

did the growly face again, which I took to mean that the building had annoyed her in some way. "When I first got here I googled all the buildings, and Knight Film Studios has a site, but for some reason my mum doesn't trust it at all."

I had no idea what googling was, or what she was talking about, and I hadn't time to find out why she or her mammy didn't like the studios.

"You go down here," I told her, trying to edge her closer to the fire escape. "And thanks for the reward offer, but give your money to a private eye instead. I'm no use to you."

"Yes, you are. You're a fighter," she said.

Sweet Mercy, was there no stopping the girl? But it didn't matter what she said now, because all I had to do was leap across to the next roof and I was free. And then maybe I could find out why the little reptile voice in my head was saying, *You're missing something, start paying attention to what's going on around you. . . .*

I took another peek at the studio parking lot. Everything was quiet except for the rolls of thunder, and the two jackals fixing their car. From the open door came the muffled roaring again, like a crowd cheering far, far away.

But this wasn't the reason my senses were stirring and saying, *Beware!* Something was making me fidgety. The thing was, I couldn't think straight around Java.

I had to get away.

"I'm not a bounty hunter or a fighter, I'm a chancer," I said, steering her to the fire escape. "I can look after myself, that's all. You wouldn't want me working for you. And that's the end of it."

But it seemed she couldn't take no for an answer. "I've done karate and tae kwon do. And I'd say you've studied some form of martial art."

"Not me, love, never." That was the truth. I'd watched martial arts being practiced and I'd taken from each of the styles the skills that I could use, but I didn't like the discipline.

"You've done some form of fighting, though," she insisted.

"OK, yes, I have," I said, just to shut her up.

"What's it called?"

I shrugged. "Call it Gypsy jive, if you like."

"Huh? Jipsi-jive?" She said it like it was Japanese. "Is it a martial art?"

She was unbelievable. I'd got a voice in my head telling me to beware, I'd got an open door that I'd got to go and investigate, but still she made me laugh. "Maybe, and the rule is we don't bow to anyone."

She nodded slowly, smiling her pixie smile back at me. "That's settled, then," she said, grasping the ladder and swinging herself over the chasm as if she was climbing down from a kid's slide in the park. "You help me find my brother and I'll pay you."

She wasn't listening to me. I had enough problems of my own without taking on anyone else's.

"Listen, I'm not a bounty hunter. I'm not going to work for you. If I were you I'd go home and sob on your daddy's knee and say you're sorry. You're very good at the pretend sobbing, believe me. Maybe Johnny will come back, maybe he won't. There's nothing you can do about it. And it sure ain't safe sleeping rough out here."

"I'm not going home," she said, in a flat little voice. But I saw her shiver and reach into her pocket with one hand and take out the bottle of Buttercup cough syrup. I understood now. Like Whitney Jade used to have her old pink blankie that she dragged around for comfort when her mammy wasn't there. Java's bottle of cough mixture was her security blanket.

I pointed over to my trailer on the edge of the green. "Go and sleep in there for the night. There's no one else in it and the door's open. You'll be safe in there."

She just stared at me with her laser-beam eyes. And that's how I left her as the first heavy drops of rain began to plop down, and I took a few quick power steps and kicked off into a jump that'd catapult me to the next roof.

I had a horrible feeling I knew what had happened to her karate-kid brother.

I woke next morning in Joe's truck with a gearshift in my ribs. It was just one more pain to add to the many I already had. My face felt like someone had stepped on it in the night, and one of my eyes wouldn't open. The pain in my head wasn't being helped by the rain drumming down on the truck's cab as though it were underneath a waterfall. Outside, Penny Park looked like it was flooding; there were puddles everywhere, and in places they'd joined up to make small lakes. I knew because I'd fallen in a fair few of them earlier in the morning.

I had no idea of the time. I looked at my cell but it'd run out of charge, so I squinted outside with my one good eye. Joe's pickup wasn't there, so maybe he'd gone to work, but that didn't tell me much. Gypsies don't work by the clock, sometimes every day is like a holiday and sometimes we work all day and all night – but only when we want to, not when a boss tells us to.

"Fwed!" called a little voice. I put a horse blanket over my head and stepped outside.

It was Whitney Jade in a Barbie plastic mac and Wellies.

"Ooer! You've been fighting again!" she said primly. "You look like a cwiminal."

A quick glance in the truck's side mirror and I saw the black eye to beat all black eyes.

"Mammy's crying," said Whitney. "Them bad boys have been again, Fwed."

"What?" I'd checked the camp in the early hours of the morning and everything had been calm.

"They've written naughty things on the side of the twailers," she said solemnly. "Daddy's really cwoss with you about it."

Ah, jeez, not again.

◆ ◆ ◆

I was getting careless. Last night my reptile brain had warned me that something was wrong, but I'd ignored it. Instead of patrolling, I'd decided to sneak into the studios, steal a few items, and get myself caught on the security cameras. That way I'd get to know the layout of the premises, which would come in useful if things turned dangerous later. It would also convince Darcus that I was all muscle and no brain, a sneak thief too stupid to avoid getting caught. And give him the opportunity to haul me inside and trap me into fighting for him.

So I'd jumped onto the second factory roof, hightailed

it down the other side, sneaked through the door left open by the jackals, and robbed the studios.

I'd got away with four totally useless credit cards, fifty pounds in cash, got my ugly mug broadcast on three of the CCTV cameras, and run into the end of a beam in the dark – hence the black eye and the headache.

The bad boy must have turned up when I'd gone to the truck and slept like the dead until morning.

I blame Java; she'd scattered my thoughts.

The bad boy had left his mark, though.

PIKE was scrawled across Crystal's trailer. **YSCU** across mine. And **MOUT** on the little tourer. If you stood far enough back it read **PIKEY SCUM OUT**. You'd have thought Hoodie could have worked out that there were three trailers and he had three words to say, and got one word on each trailer. Mind you, he'd certainly got his message across with the red spray paint. I had no proof it was Hoodie, but I hoped it was. It was bad enough one skinhead hating us without us stirring up a whole new bunch of hatred.

I stood in the rain, soaked now from head to foot, my stomach rumbling with hunger. But no amount of rain was going to wash those words away. They were the sort of words that would remain forever, even when we'd got them off with paint remover. God knows what it had done to Crystal, but I wasn't going to risk finding out.

I saw Java outside my trailer as I went by, trying to

smoke a roll-up with a coat over her head. She called out to me.

"You went into Knight Studios, didn't you?" she said as I went over. "I googled them again this morning. There's something odd, but I don't know what. Mum definitely doesn't like them." She frowned at me. "Why did you go in there?"

"No reason," I said, still not sure what she was talking about or what this google thing was.

She had the growly face on again, which I presume meant she was planning something. "Well, the Knight Film Studios site says that they help local schools with video projects and equipment, but lots of companies say that just to make out like they're helping the community or to get out of paying so much taxes. I've a good mind to phone them and make out like –"

"No way," I said quickly. "I can't tell you why, but just forget about Knight Studios."

The growly face got more growly. "You can't tell me what to do!" she said.

"I could ring the police and tell them there's a runaway living on Mrs. Bunn's shed," I replied, and then quickly began walking off toward the café, which was a wise move. The look on her face would have scared a grizzly bear now.

"You wouldn't dare!" she called out.

"I would!" I shouted back.

But not yet. Right now I needed food.

|| HH HH HH

The bell nearly shot off its spring as I opened the door of Mrs. Bunn's. I was hoping that a smell of bacon cooking might have greeted me, but the place was empty.

"Customer!" I shouted, and banged on the counter. After a long delay Mrs. Bunn appeared down a staircase, looking distracted. She had her hair in two long braids this morning, like a little milkmaid, and was wearing a ball gown. "Oh my! Our young Gypsy boy again . . ." she said despondently.

"Any chance of a brew and a cooked breakfast?" I pleaded. But she was looking back up the stairs and then back at me in a flustered way, so I gave her the Smith smile. "I'm begging you, love, anything'll do, I'm starving!"

As she dithered behind the counter, I looked through the café window to the old factory. It was quiet at the moment, but the parking lot was still full. They were the sort of cars that you wouldn't find parked in a normal street, because the first envious youth that walked by would be sure to look at all that shiny paintwork, ponder on the fact that it wasn't a fair world and that although some were born for sweet delight, others, such as himself, were born for endless night, and then scratch a key down the side.

"Breakfast?" Mrs. Bunn looked puzzled. "Oh, of course!" She clapped her hands. "I'm so sorry," she trilled. "I've had a bad morning." She put her head to one side and looked at me sweetly. "It's so difficult keeping angels alive, don't you think?"

"Absolutely," I agreed. Angel what, though? Angelfish? Angel cake? I had no idea what she was going on about, but I'd have agreed with anything she said, because now she was moving toward the food.

"Would a bacon sandwich be all right, duckie?" she asked. "Only I've got to keep my eye on . . ."

". . . the angel? No problem. A bacon butty'll be grand, love."

I sat down at one of her rickety wooden tables by the window, moved the net curtain out of the way, and kept on watching the studios. After a few minutes some more cars swung around the little park in a cavalcade. One of them was an old silver E-Type Jag with the license plate DK1. The electronic gates swung open and the motorcade drove in and parked. Darcus unfolded his mummified body from the Jag and one of the jackals leaped out of the sports car and held an umbrella over his head, like he was a VIP.

I finished my bacon sandwich and then waited. Before

long, just as I'd expected, two big goons, both of them covered in tattoos, shot out of the factory and strode straight across to the café. The bell nearly shot off its spring again as they burst in. I didn't look up until something cold touched my neck.

"Know what this is?" said one of the goons.

"Glock?" I said. Straightaway it made my skin burn and my eyes itch.

"Wise guy," he said. I think I'd ruined his surprise. I might not be much good at school, but I'm a boy, and boys know their guns, right? It might take forever to learn the times tables, but give a boy a chart of gun types and he'll know them in ten minutes. Even if his mother's one of those tree-hugger women who wouldn't let her son anywhere near a toy gun because it might turn him into a delinquent.

"Mr. Knight wants to see you," he said.

|||
||| ||| |||

"**S**tay there and don't move."

Jeez, I didn't have much choice.

The shabbiness of the outside of the old factory was a sham. As soon as the goons pushed the intercom and snarled into the CCTV camera just above it, the buzzer went and we walked into a reception area of marble and chrome. It was full of men swigging Red Bull from cans, their ties hanging loose and their shirts untucked. They were shouting to each other, but underneath their voices I could hear the sound of distant roaring. It was the same sound I'd heard last night on the roof, and I now knew where it was coming from. It was coming up from deep down below my feet.

A bell pinged and old-fashioned elevator doors creaked open opposite me, and more men spilled out into the reception space. My hackles rose. The sound of roaring was louder, and now I could tell that it was men's voices bellowing.

In front of us was the reception desk. A woman was answering the phone.

"Which school did you say you were from?" she was

saying. "Oh OK, yes, I see, you've been on our Web site. Well, yes, we did your hockey video a couple of years ago. I suppose we might have a copy here. Yes, you *could* pick it up, but I'll have to check with Mr. Knight first, if you could just hold . . ."

"And while you're at it tell Mr. Knight we got the Gypsy kid," said one of the goons.

I must have twitched because the goon jabbed me. Which set my nose itching and I sneezed a couple of times, making him jab the gun hard into the base of my skull again.

"Lighten up," I said. "I'm allergic to guns, that's all."

He ignored me, just kept the gun barrel right against my head as we waited for the receptionist to page Darcus Knight.

I felt something skitter by my legs and the goon kicked out at it, but I couldn't bend and see what it was. I thought it was a dog at the time. It disappeared between the men, who were being shepherded along by a girl I could have looked at all day. When she saw me and the goon, she beckoned us with a bejeweled finger.

She was the hottest girl I'd ever seen. She looked like someone famous, a singer in a band or an actress in a Hollywood movie. She walked to meet us as though a hundred photographers were crowding around, fighting each other to take pictures of her. She looked like she should be walking down a red carpet, dripping with diamonds. She had baby blue eyes and blond hair down to her waist, and she didn't look like any girl I'd ever seen before.

"So, this is the thief!" she said, looking me up and down as though I were a prize dog she'd got to judge. So far she was the only one in the place who'd smiled at me. She tapped me on the cheek. "You've really got that bad-boy thing going for you, haven't you?"

I couldn't think of a thing to say.

"I'm Rachel," she said. She glanced at the goon. "Darcus is on his way."

I stood and waited with my heart going nineteen to the dozen. If I'd just been challenged to a fight, I'd have been as steady as a rock, but stand me in front of a girl like this and I'm a goner.

"Ah, nice to see you again, Freedom!" The crowds parted and Darcus swooped down on us like a bird of prey.

"You'll pay for this, mister," I said, playing the angry Gypsy boy for all it was worth. Really I was spending most of my time taking in everything around me. How many paces it took to get from the door to reception. How many steps to the elevators. Where the emergency exits were, and whether they were alarmed. You never know when this sort of detail will come in useful.

Darcus grasped my hand with his freezing-cold claw. I pulled away from him, it was like being touched by Death. "You are an absolute treasure!" He beamed.

"Mr. Knight?" said the receptionist. "That school we

did the hockey video for, they want to send someone down for an extra copy, it's urgent –" she began.

Darcus gave a smug smile. "Why, tell them that would be no problem!" He looked over at me and gave his death grin. "Pillars of the community, that's what we are. Let's keep everybody sweet and everything out in the open. Nothing to hide here, right?"

"So who're all these people?" I butted in, looking at the men milling around.

"Guests at another of our little ventures. One that isn't quite so open as our educational videos," said Darcus.

He waved a hand at the crowd around us, which was slowly disappearing, either down in the elevator or out into the parking lot.

"We're just changing from the night show to the day," he said, as though I were a visiting guest he was entertaining. "So it's always busy around this time." He leaned toward me, his old destroyed voice no match for the noise in reception. A chill was gradually seeping over us. Darcus emanated cold like a freezer with the door left open.

"This is a high-energy place, Freedom, so we like to keep our guests moving, too much adrenaline washing through their veins to leave them standing around. That's why you have so many fights and arguments at airports. Never leave overexcited people waiting, is our company motto."

"This ain't no proper company," I said roughly. "What is it? Illegal fights? You doing bare-knuckle?"

Darcus's ancient watery eyes glittered. "Oh, my boy! You have no idea!" He gave me the sort of smile a vampire would give its victims before draining them of blood.

I lowered my head and glared at both Darcus and the goon. It wasn't hard to make myself look at them with loathing.

"You're gonna regret this," I said. "This is kidnap."

Darcus raised an eyebrow at me. "So you'll be calling the police and reporting us?"

"Yeah, too right," I bluffed, playing my part of a rogue with more muscle than thinking power.

"Even though we have your little excursion into my studios caught on security camera." A photo printout appeared in his hand. It was a freeze-frame from a CCTV camera, showing me rifling through a desk. I tried to look guilty. It wasn't hard – lately it seemed to be my default expression. Even the angry body language I was faking was coming easily to me.

I stared furiously into space for a moment or two and then started to pace about like a caged tiger. The goon immediately came forward with the gun raised, but Darcus gave one of his tiny signals and he stopped.

"You don't know!" I burst out. "You don't know what it's like being me!" I cracked the knuckles on one of my hands, making Darcus wince delicately. "Everyone's always on my tail, telling me I'm wrong . . . Jeez, my family, the police, everybody . . ." I raised my fists. That got the goon twitching about with his gun again. "It's like I'm gonna explode. And all anybody ever says to me is 'Keep out of trouble.'" I paced some more. Darcus watched me, his yellowing eyes dancing. "So go on, ring the police, see if I care. Jeez, it's only a matter of time before they take me in, anyway." I stopped, breathing heavily. I'd planned that little speech while I'd been eating my bacon sandwich, and I'd said it convincingly. Too convincingly. I swear it's how I feel most of the time.

"Oh, I don't use our boys in blue," said Darcus smoothly. He was fiddling with his necktie now, pretending not to be that interested in this wild Gypsy boy in front of him. But I could tell he was watching every move and twitch I made. I don't think I was the only body language expert in the room. Which was fine by me; I'd never give myself away with a careless gesture.

He nodded toward the goon. "We have our own ways of punishing people." He put his hands together in a steeple and smiled. "But why don't you calm down and tell me what's the matter?"

"I've been getting in a lot of bother lately," I said. I started pacing again, but not so angrily this time. The goon gave a twitch but soon settled down, leaning his back against the wall and watching me. "I'm too good a fighter, see, and blokes take a dislike to me, and then I cause my family lots of bother. Now they're fed up with me. But I don't care, I've got my own plans."

I looked up. Darcus's eyes were shining now. "I tell you what," he said, with his steepled fingers to his lips, as if he were contemplating something he'd never thought of before, although I knew this was a lie. "I'd like to give you a chance to redeem yourself, to join our fighting team."

"Listen, mister," I said, acting like I'd seen a ray of light at the end of a tunnel. "I can fight anyone, anytime, that's no problem. You want to do a deal?" This was working exactly as I'd hoped it would. I pointed to the photo in his hands. "I think we can come to an arrangement." I began moving again, as though I couldn't stay still.

Darcus tapped his steepled fingers against his lips. "Slowly. Not so fast. First I'll have to give you a little tryout, see if you're as good as I think you are."

"What makes you think I'm any good at all?" I said suspiciously, just to catch him out. I stopped and faced him.

He smiled, showing some disastrous teeth, and said, "You have the look of a wild boy, and my punters like that in a young fighter. Come, let's see what you can do."

He put a bony arm around my shoulders and steered me through the men still in reception. They took little notice of me, but there was a lot of handshaking with Darcus.

"Newbie?" said a big-bellied businessman in a suit, glancing at me. I snarled, and the goon jabbed with the gun to remind me to behave.

"Maybe," said Darcus, and they shared a smile, the man looking me up and down.

Now I knew what a horse felt like on the selling ground at Appleby Fair.

◆ ◆ ◆

I entered the gym by being shoved from behind by the goon and falling through the doors.

The place was lined with mirrors and full of the usual weight machines and barbells. In the middle was a boxing ring. I began to sweat. Around the ring there was an arrangement of video cameras on a sleek rig. If Darcus was into videoing the fights in the ring, he was making sure he got a shot of every angle, although it might've had something to do with the computer set up by the ropes. A pale man with pale hair and eyes, like a maggot that'd never seen the sun, was clicking away at it.

"OK, strip down to shorts only," said Darcus. "And we'll see what you can do." He threw me a pair of green satin boxer's shorts with a sledgehammer embroidered across the back in gold. I put them on. Thank God no one would see me in them.

I jogged around a bit, getting my muscles warmed up. The maggoty man began fixing surgical tape to a bunch of tiny metal gadgets. Some of the fighters working out at the weights gave me sidelong looks. They were a strange bunch: tattooed men with massive barrel chests and faces puffed with bruises, tall black guys stripped to the waist and laced with scars, old boxers with broken noses and dazed eyes, and boys so skinny you could see the ripping on their muscles.

"Stand still," said the maggoty man.

He began fixing the tiny metal gadgets onto my head, body, and legs with sticky tape.

"What's this all about?" I said.

The man glanced up. "Motion capture and analysis." He held up one of the little gadgets. "I put these sensors on all your joints and limbs, the cameras capture the movements you make and the power behind your punches, and we get a 3-D image on the screen."

"Kushti," I said. I looked at the boxing ring and began to sweat again. "Do I have to fight in the ring? I don't like rings."

For me, fighting is not about thumping away at someone's head with gloves. It's mostly about moving fast, being smarter than your opponent, and *not* fighting. But in a ring that was impossible.

He pointed to the video rig. "'Fraid so. That's where the cameras are set up. They pick up the signals from the sensors and show us a complete picture of your style, how hard you punch, how you move." He glanced at me. "It'll tell us whether you're good enough for us." He turned the computer around. A matchstick figure was standing there. I waved an arm. The matchstick figure waved back. "That's you," said the man.

But I'd stopped listening, because I'd seen something unbelievable. Just when I was congratulating myself on getting this far into Darcus's organization with only a black eye, Java strolls into the gym, smiling.

||||
|||| |||| ||||

I couldn't believe the girl! She'd actually found a way to follow me in here. And as far as I could tell she'd done it without a single scratch, unlike me.

She was in a school uniform with a tie and a pleated skirt, although I'm not sure that school uniforms are supposed to be that short. She still had the Docs on, though.

My heart gave a thump, and I felt sweat break out on my forehead. Anyone might have seen her over at the trailers and know that we were acquainted. Had she any idea of the danger she was putting herself into? One wrong move and it wouldn't just be her brother who disappeared off the face of the earth.

The receptionist followed her through, looking a bit dazed. "Um, Mr. Knight, this is the girl who rang about the hockey video. You don't happen to know where we keep the community video copies, do you?"

Darcus narrowed his yellow eyes. "Edit suite," he snapped, then remembered he was really supposed to be a kindly old uncle, even though he looked like one that'd been dead for months and starting to decay. He pasted his idea of a smile onto his face, and aimed it at Java. "Always happy to help, my dear."

"Thank you!" said Java, all bright eyes and pixie charm. Feet together primly, chin up, she held out her hand to Darcus. "Mr. Knight, I'm captain of the hockey team, and I'd like to thank you so much for taking an interest in our school. My head teacher was wondering if I could possibly have a look around. It would help my media studies so much!"

"My pleasure!" Darcus lied. "Here to help the local community, that's our motto." He waved a hand around. "We're filming a series of martial arts videos at the moment." You had to hand it to Darcus; he'd found the perfect cover for his activities.

He put an arm around my shoulders. "And this young man is about to take part in a sparring match." He adjusted a couple of the sensors taped to my arms, then inclined his head gracefully toward the computer. "We have a very sophisticated movement analyzer, and Freedom here is going to be our guinea pig. If you'd like to take a seat, I could answer a few of your questions while Freedom shows us his particular fighting skills –"

"I don't want to fight in the ring," I said, trying to deflect Darcus's interest back to me. One wrong comment from Java and she could blow the whole thing.

"Why?" said Darcus, his smile fading. His arm tightened around my shoulders.

"It's a Smith thing," I said. "I'm like my great-great-great-granddaddy, I don't like boxing rings. I swear to God he once had to fight a wild animal in a cage. After that he couldn't stand being closed in, or even having ropes around the fight area. It's the same with me."

Darcus's eyes danced madly again.

"Tell me more! This ancestor of yours sounds fascinating. Hercules in the lion's den, what an amazing thing!"

Which was odd, because it *was* a lion my great-great-great-granddaddy fought, and he *was* called Hercules. Seems like Darcus had done more than just stalk me all those years ago. Seems like he'd done a bit of research. But there wasn't time to figure it out, because there was the sound of a wild scuffle at the gym door, and a shout that was quickly cut off. I caught a glimpse of one of the jackals I'd seen yesterday, with dark cropped hair and bleached, spiky bangs. He was complaining that someone had taken his cap.

"Excuse me while I get your opponent," said Darcus, turning icy again, all pretense of being kind and jolly gone. He signaled to the goon to follow him, leaving me and Java alone in the gym.

I watched them go.

"Nice shorts!" said Java innocently.

I gave her my best bad-boy scowl. "Nice uniform."

It wasn't. She'd cobbled it together from stuff she'd

found in the trailer. That was Joe's tie, and one of Whitney's skirts, going by the length of it. And she'd found a navy sweater of mine.

"Our Lady of Sorrows High School?" I said.

Her eyes widened in surprise. "Do you know it?"

"Yes," I said. "I was there once . . ."

"At a girls' school?"

". . . with my hands behind my head as the police frisked me and checked my pockets. We were camped on the field next door, and I decided to climb up the clock tower for the hell of it, and they called the police." I grinned at her. "They removed me from school premises."

That got me another frown. Then she looked away and frowned at everyone else in the gym.

"Does this company really make videos to do with fighting? Is everyone here a fighter?" she said. I could almost see the cogs whirring in her mind. She was suspecting what I suspected: that her karate-champ brother was in here. But she was confused, I could see it in her eyes. She knew that her mammy had been right and that this was no ordinary film company.

"Leave it," I muttered. But I didn't get the chance to warn her not to ask any more questions.

"Got any candy, mister?" said the tiniest voice ever, by my feet.

The makeshift boxing ring next to me was elevated maybe three feet off the ground, and the space underneath had been masked off with canvas. I saw the canvas twitch. I bent down, pretending to tie my sneaker, and pulled the canvas aside.

Jeez, it hadn't been a dog scuttling between our legs earlier. I wished to God it had been.

Hiding under the ring was a small boy, maybe the same size as Whitney Jade. He had a bandanna around his scruffy head, and someone had roughly fashioned him a little guerrilla outfit by cutting off the sleeves of a bigger camouflage jacket and tying rope around it. I don't think anyone had given him a bath for ages.

They take kids and they train them up, Wren had said. *They never know anything else but the Bear Pit.*

The boy held out a filthy little paw.

If you see any of these kids, don't get involved. Play it like you don't care. Don't give yourself away.

"Sorry, kid," I said softly. "I'll get you some next time."

I twitched the canvas aside a bit more. There was a sort of nest inside, made of clothes and gym towels, the sort of thing that chimps make in the wild out of leaves. And there was a trail of old potato chip bags and Red Bull cans leading to it. Jeez, it was a wonder the kid hadn't got rickets and the shakes with a diet of salt, fat, and caffeine.

"What's your name?" I whispered again. All I could see was the sparkle from a small pair of eyes watching me from far back in the darkness.

"Ant?" said the tiny voice, as though he wasn't sure.

"Oh my God, it's a little boy!" said Java, bending down beside me. "What's he doing under there? He's filthy! Why the hell is this place letting a small boy get in that state?"

I grabbed her arm and dragged her up, letting the canvas drop down over the little boy's nest.

"Later. He's coming back."

Darcus was coming toward us with his beautiful assistant, Rachel, and the jackal with the bleached bangs.

I sized him up as an opponent.

He was my height, not much older than me, and still wearing his sleeves rolled right up to show his muscles. But he wasn't blank-faced like he had been yesterday; now he was straining at the leash, and I don't think he got that sort of energy from knickerbocker glories.

My old boxing coach would've been disgusted. He'd taught me that you win by reading the other fighter's body language, by getting into his mind – and I'd swear this guy had taken performance-enhancing steroids.

"I want you to put the newbie through his paces," Darcus told him, pointing to me.

The jackal was bouncing on his toes. "Leon took my cap. I want my lucky cap," he said in a stubborn voice. "I *need* my lucky cap."

"You shouldn't go anywhere near Leon, I've warned you before, boy. Now get into the ring and keep it clean," I heard Darcus say. He put a hand briefly over the boy's mouth, as though he was giving a horse a sugar lump.

The jackal crunched on something, then shook himself, spat on the floor, and snorted. All he needed was a ring through his nose and a hoof scratching the ground and he'd be a bull ready to charge.

"My skin's on fire," he said, his eyes like black pools. "Come on, Gypsy. Fight me."

He ducked under the ropes and bounced into the ring. He bounced some more and then stroked his bangs to make sure they were standing upright. I supposed he wanted to look good for when he beat me. I pretended to tie up my other sneaker, flexing my muscles and getting myself ready. I took a few deep breaths to steady my breathing. My hand shook slightly as I tied the bow and did a knot on top, making sure the ends of the laces were the same length. Then a bloke with his hair shaven to within a millimeter of its life came over. He wasn't here to fight, but to referee, it seemed, because he said, "Get in the ring, I haven't got all day."

I nodded and ducked under the ropes, trying to make the best of it, but I didn't like it, and all I could think about was Hercules and how I'd always wished I could have met him. I was his heir, right enough. He'd been the same age as me at his first fight, squaring up to the reigning champion – Tom Gaskin, the Man of Granite – and knocking him out cold in two seconds. From that day on, wherever men gathered together to scratch a mark on the ground and two fighters squared up to each other, Hercules Smith was the king. But he never set foot in a ring; he just wouldn't do it.

He would have understood why my hands were shaking when the ref strapped a pair of thin half-gloves onto my fists.

The ref slapped me on the back. "Fight."

Then it was too late to worry about anything. I got my hands up and started doing some jabs, warming up, taking deep breaths, feeling the sensors on all my joints. The iron-pumpers had stopped and were clustering around. The circle of eyes made it worse.

"Stuff it!" said the jackal. "I'm on fire. Fight me!" And he bounced around, jabbing out at thin air.

I got onto the balls of my feet and started to move.

There was nothing in here that I hadn't faced on the street, but that old gut feeling of being trapped wouldn't listen to reason. People think I'm fearless. I'm not. I have a million and one fears: that a bad bloke will get hold of the little girls, that a plane will come over one day and bomb us, that a skinhead will finally succeed in burning the pikeys, that a black car will come and take me in the night. Even heights, they scared me when I was a kid, so what do I do now? I spend my life up on the roofs, daring myself to be scared, making things edgy.

I took a deep breath. *Feel the fear and do it*, I told myself.

Darcus had got one of his men to pull three chairs up to the ringside, beside the computer. Java, Rachel, and Darcus were just feet away, staring at me. I began sweating.

Me and the jackal were circling each other, like two wild animals sizing each other up. Time slowed, and every little sound became crystal clear. Over to my right I could hear Darcus giving Java a rundown on what was happening.

"Why aren't they wearing proper boxing gloves?" she was saying urgently. The frown was back. Jeez, maybe she was worried about me. "They'll hurt their hands otherwise, won't they?"

Darcus leaned close. "They have martial arts lightweight gloves. These give a little protection to the knuckles, but they're open so the fighters can grapple. And, in any case, normal boxing gloves are far more dangerous than bare hands."

Darcus was right about that at least. A fighter with

heavy gloves and loads of tape wrapped around his hands can hardly feel the blows he's throwing, so he hits as hard as he can. Only problem is that he's hitting another man's jaw, and jawbones are not nearly as hard as his gloved fists. But when a man is bare-knuckle fighting, he has to take care of his hands. He feels every blow and so he doesn't hit as hard, not unless he wants to bust his knuckles open. So says my Uncle Shady, anyway.

Java didn't look convinced. She continued to watch me, her eyes like headlights now.

We started to spar. I didn't move too quickly to begin with; I wanted to watch him closely.

"I'm flying," he said in a jittery voice. He got in a couple of jabs, one I ducked, one that caught me a glancing blow. But like I've said, I've got a chin made of steel.

"Bet that hurt," I said as he swayed back, shaking his fist.

"Fight!" said the ref, shoving me. "Not talk."

So we began to fight properly. Out of the corner of my eye I could see Darcus and Java looking from the computer to me and back again. My little stick figure on the screen must have been giving them the results they wanted, because the maggot man was nodding and smiling to himself.

Twenty seconds in and the jackal says, "Damn you, I

want my lucky cap," again, and I knew he was worried. The referee shoved him this time.

"Fight on!"

It turned out he wasn't that good. He was just a machine that kept coming and coming. He kept looking around as though waiting for the other jackals to step in and help him. He was a pack hunter, not a lone wolf. I had to spend more time not hurting him than I did shielding myself from some of his punches.

I risked a glance toward my audience. I couldn't tell what golden girl Rachel was thinking. Her face was blank. I suppose she'd seen it all before. But Java must have needed some comfort, because she was sneakily taking a sip from her Buttercup syrup.

At which point the jackal hit me on the nose, and this was swiftly followed by the canvas coming up and hitting me in the face, and then the world went black . . .

. . . and I thought it was the dead of night and I was small again, huddled by the roadside with Crystal trying to shield me. And I saw Darcus's corpselike face leaning down over me, and I felt a pain in my arm. Then a wheezing old voice said, "This should work: a sample fresh from Hercules' heir. If this doesn't cure Leon, nothing will."

Then his face faded into the dark night as a sponge full of water hit me in the face.

I blinked.

"Maybe you're ready to start fighting again now," said the ref.

I picked myself off the floor and shook my head. I'd been knocked out before but I'd never had a nightmare like that. Even if it was another piece of the puzzle, it'd left me wanting to run out of the gym, onto a rooftop, and not stop running until I'd left Darcus well behind.

I glanced across at him. He was watching me avidly. So was Java, but she had her hand across her mouth in horror. The jackal was standing by the ref, looking pleased with himself. Even the men watching from the ringside had begun to move away, like they'd seen enough.

To tell the truth, I'd had enough as well, so I moved fast, fast even for me, and I tripped the jackal before anyone even noticed me move, and got an armlock on.

After a few seconds he lifted his face from the canvas. "I want my cap," he grunted again.

But I only let go when he tapped the ground for mercy.

"OK, you can go and get your cap now," I said.

As he stumbled away there was the sound of applause. It was Darcus. Beside him Rachel was smiling at me. Java still had her hand over her mouth, but she was watching the computer screen where the maggoty man was tapping away, shaking his head.

Darcus looked at the screen. "Well?" he said.

The maggoty man glanced across at me, and then

looked up at Darcus. "Oh, he's the one, all right! We've found him again at last; he's definitely got the gene. No mistaking." He pointed to the screen. "Phenomenal results. Look!" And he shook his head like he couldn't believe it. But Darcus shot him a warning look. "That's enough," he said quietly, like he didn't want others overhearing.

He signaled to the goon to escort Java out. Amazingly, she went without any fuss, giving me a startled look as she went by.

"My boy!" said Darcus, coming up to me and handing me a towel. I wiped the trickle of blood from my sore nose. "You didn't disappoint at all!"

He said nothing else, just reached inside his suit and pulled out a bundle of cash. He counted it out in twenty-pound bills before me on the computer table, as though he was setting out fortune-telling cards like my Great-Granny Kate used to do in her younger days, when she got up to hanky-panky.

"I bet that's more money than you've seen in a long time," he said.

I'd seen lots of cash around before, of course. Travelers work in a cash economy. No one's going to give bank accounts or credit cards to people without addresses, so Lord knows what'll happen to us if they ever abolish money and work only with bits of plastic.

"Last time I saw this much cash was when I handed it over to Greenacres, when my daddy bought an ill-fated bit of land for us just outside the town," I said bitterly. "We were told we could live on the plot, but it turned out to be unusable, except as a home for some precious newts that everyone cared about more than us. So all that money was wasted." I looked at the cash greedily. I didn't have to act. "I could desperately use some more cash."

Darcus nodded as though he understood exactly what it was like to be cheated out of your life savings and know that there was nothing you could do about it. But I doubted that he would ever be in that situation. When you've got goons with guns around, things like that tend not to happen.

"You'll get all this after your first fight," he said. "If you agree to move in with us and dedicate your life to our fight, our special fight. And I'm not talking about the amateur stuff up here, not the sparring and the boxing." He tilted his head back and watched me very carefully. "You need discipline, boy, and you'll find it with us. Other people might not like your skills, but here they will earn you a fortune."

That was the second person to tell me I needed discipline and then offer to be the one who'd give it to me. No wonder I liked to deal with life alone.

I picked up one of the twenties.

"Kushti," I said, and it wasn't hard to act like I was tempted. I leaned closer to the money, enjoying the sight and smell of it, until a drip of blood from my nose fell on it, marking it with a scarlet splash like a flower. Blood money.

The truth was, I could look at it and smell it all I liked, but it would never be mine. After the first fight I would be blowing the whistle on Darcus and the Bear Pit, and calling Wren in. I'd never get my hands on that money.

I was doing this for redemption. I was thinking that if I proved I was good, then Clunk wouldn't die, even though I knew that the world didn't work like that.

"I'll fight for you," I lied.

Darcus licked his thin dry lips. "I'm talking about real fighting in front of real fight fans. I'm talking about a whole new world."

"Extreme fighting?" I said.

He nodded.

"Well, I sure as hell hope they're more extreme than the last guy," I said scornfully.

Darcus looked like it was his birthday. "That's the ticket!" he croaked, his voice breaking even more than usual as he realized he was going to get what he wanted. Me.

He collected the twenty-pound bills up in a stack and I followed his every move, like a dog watching a bone. I couldn't take my eyes off the bills. There's nothing like the feeling of having a bundle of cash held together by a rubber band in your pocket. You feel like you can be king of the world then. "You'll earn more money than you ever dreamed of," he said, watching the greed on my face. "But you must come to us wholeheartedly, and make us your family from now onward."

I shrugged. "OK by me. To tell you the honest truth, I think my sister'll be glad to see the back of me." The lie came easily, but then I realized that maybe it wasn't so much of a lie anymore. "And my sister's husband hates me and wants me out. I'm fed up with them all, anyway," I continued. "I'm nearly sixteen and I want to live my own life."

Darcus held up a warning hand. "You must tell no one where you're going. If people start knocking here and we have to move, you'll be punished. It's a hard life here, but you'll make yourself a fortune."

"OK," I said, like I had nothing to lose.

"Our fight is beyond the law. Does that bother you?"

I looked scornfully at him. "No!"

His Adam's apple jumped as he gave an involuntary little gulp of anticipation. "Good. Are you prepared to trust me in all things and give yourself over to the glorious fight, the fight that never stops?"

He steepled his hands together, fingertip against fingertip. He was calm, confident; he knew I was in his power. He had me now, or so he thought. I looked at the money.

"OK," I said.

And without even realizing what he was doing, he lifted his steepled hands and put them behind his head.

It looked like he'd crowned himself, as though he was a king.

"Welcome to the Bear Pit," he said.

I spat on my hand, and watched him wince. He might look like he was decaying, he might be involved in fights that were full of blood and gore, but he was a dandy, you could tell by his spotless suit and the soft mottled hands with their clean nails.

"Let's seal the deal Gypsy style," and I held out my hand.

Job done.

◆ ◆ ◆

It's easy, Wren had said. *Just go over to the studios and ask for a job. He'll take you straight in when he sees who you are.*

Yeah, sure, but where's the Gypsy style in that? So I'd done it my way instead.

Different technique, that's all. Same outcome. Plus a black eye and a bloody nose.

‖‖ |
‖‖ ‖‖ ‖‖

The same rain was falling, tepid like bathwater. And the thunder had come back, circling the park as though we were in the eye of the storm. But there was no calm around our little camp.

I could hear my sister shouting before I got anywhere near.

There was a police car outside the trailers, and a policewoman inside, taking notes, managing to make a fuss over the little girls and the baby but glare at me. I knew her from the other times we'd stopped in the town. She was hard but fair, and usually on our side. This time she kept looking at me as though I was dangerous.

"Dear God, just look at him! He's been fighting again!" said Crystal in disbelief when she saw my nose.

The policewoman shook her head and tutted at me. "If you stayed out of trouble, maybe your sister wouldn't have all this grief with thugs. You're a burden, that's what you are."

Burden. It was only a word, spoken casually, but it repeated itself again and again in my mind, and once

122

more my life changed lanes without me knowing. There was a wrong turn over the horizon, and now I was heading straight for it.

But one thing was for sure, I'd never seen my sister so upset. "Is there any way we could get a house, love?" she said to the policewoman. "I can't stand it any longer."

Jeez, I couldn't believe I'd heard right when she said that. Putting a traveler into a house is like turning a black man white. But one look at Crystal's face made me keep my mouth shut. If I hadn't been in so much trouble I'd have been proud of myself for staying quiet again.

The policewoman didn't seem to think so, though, and gave me another black look.

"You'll be all right for the next few weeks, anyway. We've had orders from on high that it's OK for you to stay in Penny Park for a while, and we're to let you be for a few weeks."

That would be on Wren's say-so, I thought.

The policewoman tickled Little Frisco under his dribbly chin. "And in the meantime, I'll try and get you a house."

Crystal managed a weak smile. "We're proud people. We don't want to live in houses, we want to live our way, but it's getting too much for my nerves. Try your best, love."

But Joe, who'd just come back from shifting and watering the horses, heard this and scowled at her. He also found time to squeeze in a dark look for me – surprise, surprise.

"We don't need a house!" he said.

"Too right, you tell her," I said, but Joe pushed angrily by me and threw a couple of halters on the table.

"I mean we need our own land, we need to get off the roadside, give the girls somewhere proper to grow up," he said. "I'm sick of the city and the skinheads."

The heat in the trailer seemed to rise, as though we were in a pressure cooker about to go off.

The policewoman stood up, looking wary. I think she'd seen enough family rows to know when one was about to start.

"We want our own place! If I could just get on with my work in peace," said Joe, gazing daggers at me, "then I might get the money together."

"What, and get cheated again?" I said to him, sick of being blamed all the time for everyone else's misfortunes. I turned to the policewoman. "You know what they do now? If we bid for a piece of land, the people living nearby outbid us, until we can't afford it no more. And they buy the land for themselves, and sell it later to someone who isn't a traveler, and everybody wins except us."

"That's just wild talk," said the policewoman, but she looked away. She knew it was true, it was happening all the time.

"We don't need a house," muttered Joe. "We need land."

"And where are we going to get the money from to buy it?" said Crystal, her eyes flashing now, but more from tears than from anger.

"OK, let's everybody calm down," said the policewoman. I think she thought she was about to have a domestic on her hands.

"I'll help," I said. "I could bring in some money." I just wanted them to stop arguing, for everything to stop being my fault. I'd got a pain in my gut, the sick feeling you get when you know things are going wrong and can only get worse.

Joe gave me a look that withered me. "Yeah, that'd be the day. The only thing you bring in is trouble."

"Leave him alone," said Crystal.

The temperature rose another couple of degrees, until Joe hunched his shoulders and pulled his jacket up around his neck, and then slammed out and went over to the horsebox. Crystal jogged the baby about and stared angrily out at the rain.

"I'd make myself scarce for a while if I were you, sonny," said the policewoman.

Too right I would. Maybe I'd make myself scarce for good.

||||| ||
||||| ||||| |||||

"**N**o one should be able to strike that fast!"

Seems like Java had moved into my trailer, and now there was no peace for me anywhere.

"You fight like you're invincible."

"I got knocked out!" I said.

Java tapped her foot. "That's because you got distracted. Not because your opponent was better than you." She looked me up and down. "They said you've inherited your skills from your ancestors."

Wren had called it the Hercules gene and said that in the wrong hands it could be dangerous. That's why Darcus wanted it. Seems like I was the only one who didn't want my inheritance. At the moment it was nothing but trouble – for instance, I had a feeling my nose'd never be the same shape again.

"What exactly is a gene?" I said, wringing a wet washcloth out in the sink and dabbing my nose gingerly with it.

Java stopped pacing. "Oh, we did this in science. They're small segments of DNA that make up the chromosomes in our cells. It's our genes that contain all the information about who we are, like what color skin we're born with, or the color of our hair. Sometimes there are mutant genes, and then all sorts of things can go wrong."

Trust Java to be a fountain of knowledge. But I didn't want to hear any more, especially about mutant genes, because I think she'd been trying to say that mutant genes could turn you into a freak. And that's what I felt like most of the time.

"That reward you mentioned? How much would it be for?" I said, trying to get Whitney Jade off my knee. She was helping me dab my nose with the wet cloth, but it was causing more harm than good.

"Five thousand pounds," Java said promptly.

I thought she was joking to begin with. "Where are you going to get five grand?" I said, and she looked away.

"I've got it already. It's mine."

"Fair enough," I said. Five thousand pounds wasn't enough, but it was a start. Crystal and Joe would have their land.

"Please, Fwed! Let me have a go on the tom tooter!"

Java had a laptop out on the table, as part of her takeover of my space. She'd pulled it out of her backpack like a magician producing a rabbit from a hat, and Whitney Jade was fascinated.

"Cash?" I said. Checks would be no use, I had no bank account. "Cash, if I can find him?"

"Cash." Java tip-tapped a few buttons and a game

sprang up on the screen. Whitney Jade leaped toward it like she'd been put under a magic spell.

And now that she was out of the way, Java could come over, all intense. "So, you'll work for me?"

I shook my head. "I don't work *for* people, but if I find your brother for you, the price as agreed will be five thousand pounds, cash on delivery. Shake?"

I didn't spit on my hand this time, you understand. It was like shaking hands with a bird.

She shook, and then began fixing me with her blazing eyes.

"So Johnny is in the film studios, then?" she said.

I swear, now that I'd got the money sorted out, all I wanted to do was get some sleep. The alpha waves in my brain kept kicking in.

My old coach always told me not to worry about my fists but to learn everything I could about my brain. He said that was the way to beat any opponent. That and body language. So I'd taken an interest in both. And at that moment, my alpha waves were telling me to get a bit of sleep. I think it was a case of my body wanting nothing more to do with today.

I sat down on the bench and my eyes began to close of their own accord.

"Freedom?"

"Mmm?"

"He is, isn't he?"

I tried to sit up straight. "Yes, I think he is."

"I knew it!" She began pacing up and down the trailer again. "My mum told me Darcus and Rachel were bad."

"I don't think Rachel is part of it," I said.

Java gave me a scornful look. "Just because she's beautiful, it doesn't mean she's good."

The thing is, it made me even more tired just watching her pacing up and down, so I closed my eyes again. But that turned out to be a bad idea, because straightaway Clunk began running across my mind. I forced my eyes open.

"Are they staging illegal fights in there?" she demanded. "Is that why Johnny has broken contact with me? And why was that little boy, Ant, hiding under the ring? What's going on in there?"

Dear Lord, she had no idea. It was another world altogether, according to Wren. So I didn't answer.

"Freedom!"

My elbow slipped off the table, jolting me awake again. I nearly got a split chin to go with the black eye and bloody nose.

"Yes. And I'll get him out," I said, just to shut her up so that I could go to sleep.

"Thanks. You won't be on your own. I'll help you."

I sat up when she said that.

"No way. I work alone," I said. "I've already got a way in. People who do bare-knuckle fights are not nice people.

I'll go in there alone and see what's what, and then I'll come and tell you."

I didn't want other people around me in a dangerous situation, because then half my mind would be on keeping them safe, and I'd worry that they might get hurt, which would give me something else to feel guilty about.

"But it sounds too dangerous –"

"No. It's OK, I've got police backup –"

That's what happens when you talk while you're falling asleep. You blurt out things that maybe shouldn't be blurted out.

"The police know? The police know about it and didn't tell me that Johnny –?"

So I told her everything, just to shut her up. Wren would have narrowed his eyes and lit a cigar in disgust. I told her all about Darcus, and the fight that never stops, and the kids who grow up in it, and the fighters who never leave the Bear Pit. And how Phoenix wanted me to work for them and close the fight down. And she said, "The police don't employ boys!" and I said, "You tell them that," which made her get that look in her eye again, like she thought I was something special when it came to fighting. But I ignored it and said that she should listen to me before she interrupted, because I wasn't actually working for the police, but I had to prove to everyone that I was a good guy because there'd been an accident that made me look bad. That this was going to be my saving grace.

"Why didn't anyone tell me this before?" she said, hugging herself.

"Because kids who go into the Bear Pit don't often come out," I said.

"But you're going to get Johnny out ..." The frown had come back, complete with the angry growling face. She looked like a worried bear cub. "I've got to ask Mum about this," she said, and then sat back and closed her eyes.

Contacting the spirit world seemed to be much easier than trying to get your cell phone to work: A second or two later she opened her eyes again. This time they were blazing.

"It's a bit muddled, but I think Mum is trying to tell me that he's OK, but he needs rescuing quickly." She stood up and began pacing again. "I have to think of a way to get in there and get him out."

"If he's there, *I'll* get him," I said. I hesitated, but in the end I decided to be honest with her. "He might not be the same. Darcus has some sort of hold on their minds. Whether anyone can recover from that is another matter."

She narrowed her eyes. "They use drugs?"

I shrugged. "Steroids, I think. They're performance enhancers, but they can have side effects, like 'roid rage.

And Darcus is an expert in mind control techniques. He could be controlling Johnny –"

"Duh! I don't care. We can deal with that later, I just want him back." She folded her arms and sat back. She might act tough, but underneath I could tell she was only just holding it together. Her brother gone, her mammy just a voice in her head, a daddy who didn't care two hoots.

And inside I couldn't stop myself thinking that maybe I *could* ask her out, have her as my girl. And it was vexing, because thoughts like that were alien to me. Not because I didn't want a girl – I did, even though I was useless with girls – but because stuff like that belonged to other people, not me. I ran alone, courted risk, got a kick out of pushing myself to the limit. Girls weren't for me. Java made me catch my breath, but I had to put ideas like that out of my mind.

"I've got an idea that might help," she said, breaking into my thoughts.

"Leave it. There's nothing you can do," I said.

Surprise, surprise, she ignored me. She wrestled the computer back from Whitney, which didn't go down well. The little girl's lip curled and her eyes went dangerously shiny.

"Here, play with this instead." Java delved into her bag and pulled out a silver box. Jeez, that bag was a bottomless pit of delights by the look of it.

"Nintendo DS," said Java, handing it over. "Much

better for little girls. Look, you can adopt a sausage dog in this game!"

The lip stopped curling and Whitney settled down again happily.

Java turned back to the laptop. A few clicks later she found what she was looking for.

"Look what I've got," she said triumphantly.

‖‖ ‖‖‖
‖‖ ‖‖ ‖‖

It was an aerial view of Penny Park, taken from the top of one of the factories, by the look of it.

"I took this a couple of days ago, before you moved here. See the parchmarks?"

"Huh?"

She pointed at the screen, to the network of brown lines, rectangles, and squares that covered the grass of the park.

"It looks like the grass has died in patterns," I said. I'd seen it in cornfields when I was on top of barns. "Aliens?"

But she didn't laugh. "Seriously, we did it in archaeology at school. We went on a Roman dig and we found ruins of buildings by looking at aerial photos like this." She zoomed the picture in. I don't know how she did it, but I was impressed, because computers didn't figure in my life at all. "The grass dries out quickly where there's less soil because of buildings underneath."

I yawned, nearly snapping my jaw. "So, there's Roman ruins under the park. Hooray."

I wasn't prepared to tell her that I knew exactly what *was* under the park.

"No!" she said impatiently. "It's tunnels and underground buildings." She pointed to the screen. "And they're all leading out from the old chemical factory. They must be cellars and corridors. And there's something else. Look."

I squinted at the screen. The parchmarks showed a network of tunnels. And there was one long line that seemed to lead all the way across the park, disappear under the road, and surface again on the little patch of grass in Mrs. Bunn's yard.

"Ta-da!" she sang, hugely pleased with herself. "Secret entrance under Mrs. Bunn's yard."

"I don't think so, love," I said, feigning indifference. The last thing I wanted her doing was trying to find a way into that place. "It's probably just a drain or something leading from her cellar. I'll check it out later," I murmured as a huge wave of tiredness washed over me and my chin dropped onto my chest.

I opened one eye. The other wouldn't budge. "How much does land cost, do you think?" I said, to get her away from her treasure map.

Five grand was a handsome sum, but it was only a start. I'd need more, but I wasn't sure how much.

Darcus has plenty of money, said a wayward thought, and a picture of the money on the desk sprang into my mind. *If that's what he paid for one fight, then his fighters must earn fortunes in a year*, it whispered in my ear. But I slammed my fist onto the table and shook the thought away. That money was not for me. I must forget about it. Java's reward was a start; I had to work from there. I was the good guy now.

"I'm thinking of a piece of land around here, big enough for a couple of trailers," I said. I didn't expect her to know. It was just a displacement activity.

Java began tapping the keyboard again.

"I'm not sure of current prices," she said brightly. "But I'll look it up for you."

I swear her fingers were a blur over the keys.

"Jeez, girl, what're you doing?" I said eventually.

"Googling," she said. I hadn't understood the first time I'd heard her use that word, and I still didn't. She looked at me curiously. "You don't know about computers?"

"I learn fast," I said. "Show me." There's not much call for computers when you're on the move all the time, but if we weren't careful, us traveling people were going to get left behind.

I didn't add that my newfound interest in them might have had something to do with the fact that I had to sit right up close to her. To see what she was doing, you understand.

She showed me what she meant by googling, and how she'd looked up the Knight Film Studios Web site and found out they'd done a bit of community work with Our Lady of Sorrows High School on a hockey video, and how she'd then gone on the school Web site and checked out a few names and what uniform they wore, so that she could call Knight Studios and worm her way in without suspicion. But even though she explained it all to me, it was still no clearer than if she'd been sitting there concocting a magic spell.

So she said I'd learn better if I did it myself. I had a go with my big fists, but even messed up doing something simple like clicking the mouse when she asked me. I felt like an idiot, and it didn't help that she kept leaning close to me, so that I kept getting a waft of Buttercup syrup, and every now and again she put her hand over mine because I wasn't using the mouse right or something. It would have been perfect if it wasn't for the fact that she lived in "World A" and I lived in "World B."

"I never knew it was about phone lines, or that you could use a cell phone to get on to it," I said.

"For heaven's sake, have you been living down a hole?" she said, amazed. "I thought everyone knew about the Internet and broadband. No?"

"You're talking to someone who hasn't ever lived in a house for more than a few weeks, love," I told her. "I don't think you can get broadband when you live on the side of the road, or on the traveler sites where we spend our winters."

And she blinked and said, "Soz! I'm a dummy. It's boarding school. I forget there's other worlds besides mine."

"World A" and "World B" again, I thought. *And they never meet.*

"I never realized. I suppose you can't get a landline, never mind the Internet, if you haven't got a house," she said in a little voice.

And I thought, *Dear God, what's going to become of us in the future when everything is computerized and we travelers are the only ones left in the whole country who don't have them and can't use them?*

"We're the last untraceable people," I said as I watched her fingers flying over the keys. "If I were to disappear off the face of the earth tomorrow, no one except my family would wonder where I went. No school would check on me, no social worker, no doctor, no boss. I'm nonexistent."

And I got a jolt in my stomach. I suddenly realized that this was why Wren had chosen me. If I disappeared, who would ever wonder where I went? I would disappear off the face of the earth, just like the other cop had.

I thought maybe Java would say that it'd be a shame if I disappeared, but that was my own personal little dream. It turned out she wasn't even listening anymore, because she'd found the site she wanted.

"Here's land for sale," she said, and hit a final key

with a flourish, like a piano player playing the last note of a symphony.

There were photos and prices, prices with too many zeros.

"The value of land has shot up recently, that's why," she explained, frowning at the screen.

I should have wondered how she knew so much about land.

I looked at the prices again. Where was a traveler to get that sort of money? And, as if in answer, my eyes turned toward the studios. Yeah, right, but that was blood money. So I made myself turn away again, and just to be sure I built a brick wall in my mind between me and that cash. It wasn't for me, I was better than that.

"Mind you, this isn't the cheapest company," she continued, clicking her way through the site. "But that's my father for you, always out for the last penny."

"This is your daddy's company?" I said. I looked on the Web page, but I couldn't see the name Sparrow anywhere.

"Yep, one of the many," she said, still tip-tapping away.

"Your daddy's name's not Sparrow, though?"

"He uses Sparowski. His parents were Polish. Me and Johnny just made it simpler."

I moved along the bench; I needed some space. "Is the five grand your daddy's money?"

Java glanced over at me and bit her lip.

"I stole it," she said. "From his company."

Sweet Mercy, that startled me. "Say again?"

She took a deep breath. "I stole it from my father's company. I thought maybe I'd wimp out if the going got tough out here. And I knew I might need help, or to pay for information. Remember, I told you I couldn't go home."

And I'd thought she'd been rude to the chauffeur or something. Now I could add thief to the previous list of nicotine addict and cough-syrup drinker. There seemed to be no end to Java Sparrow's talent for getting herself into trouble.

I'd thought my course was set. I was going to help Java. I was going to do the right thing. My reward, the bounty, was going to get us land in the future.

But I couldn't take the money now. And there really was no chance that Java would ever be my girl.

She saw me backing away and misunderstood the look on my face. "Do you want me to find something cheaper?"

"What's the name of your daddy's company?" I asked.

She moved the page back to the top until the name of the Web site could be seen.

"Greenacres," she said. "Why, do you know it?"

I felt like shaking my fist at the sky and cursing fate. I meet a girl who makes my heart pound, and she turns out to be the daughter of my enemy.

‖‖‖ ‖‖‖‖ ‖‖‖ ‖‖‖ ‖‖‖

She followed me to Mrs. Bunn's. She'd got the money with her, in the backpack.

"Freedom?"

I could have given that five grand to Joe, and it would have shown him that I wasn't useless, that I could earn money. I glanced over at the studios. Remember the wall I'd built in my mind to shield myself from Darcus's blood money? Well, a whole load of bricks had just fallen from it.

"The money's here," she said. "Take it. You've got to help me find Johnny. He's all I've got."

"I can't take the money," I said.

"Why? What is it?"

"If I took money from you, there'd be too much trouble." And I told her why.

I knew the name Greenacres, I knew it well. I'd remembered it because I'd always wanted to have a word with the owner of Greenacres Ltd.

It turns out that her daddy was the one who'd cheated us, sold us land we couldn't use. Had laughed at us when we tried to get it back. Had told someone, in our court hearing, that Gypsies couldn't read and that he'd fixed the contract so we had no comeback.

"So what?" she said. "It'll serve my father right. Losing his money to you."

She'd got herself a knickerbocker glory, too. She hadn't asked for one, had asked for a coffee in a bleak voice, but Mrs. Bunn was even nuttier than usual today, and didn't seem to be on the same planet as the rest of us. She'd been up and down the stairs – tending her angel, presumably.

We sat on either side of the table and let the ice creams melt, which was a crime in itself. But it seemed that neither of us had any appetite.

"He hates Gypsies," I said. "He'll get us arrested. One day, whether you find Johnny or not, you'll go back home. And the minute your father demands to know where his money is, we'll be in trouble, whatever you say. He'll think we stole from you. There'll be recriminations against me and Crystal. And my sister's already had about as much trouble as she can stand."

"What *do* you want, then?" she said angrily.

I'd have turned away from her, if that didn't mean I'd then be facing our camp. When I'd left my trailer I'd found Crystal crying on the step, and Joe sitting in the Mitsubishi with the stereo turned right up, staring into space.

"I want a magic wand," I said. "To make everything right."

Which was a joke, because I had one, if I cared to take it. I could join the Bear Pit for real, take the money, buy Crystal the land, and to hell with the consequences. The only thing stopping me was Clunk. I had him on my conscience. No one would ever believe I didn't mean to hurt him until I proved myself to be the good guy. The wall between me and the blood money was still there, but only just.

"Take the money," she said. "Get your own back at my dad, he deserves it."

Danger!

"What?" I said.

"I said, take the —"

Danger!

"No, not you," I said. It was the reptile talking again.

"Tell me!" she said, her eyes on fire. "What can I do to make —"

"I, um, uh." And for a moment, I couldn't remember what I was doing, or what I was saying or thinking. Then the hairs on the back of my neck stood on end, and I thought, *Whoa, here we go again.* And all the colors around me got very bright, and everything in sight got so detailed that it seemed like I could see every molecule in the universe as clear as day, and every little noise in the café became loud, even the tiny little clicks of Mrs. Bunn's water heater chuntering to itself and the tapping of her feet as she walked about.

And then came the rushing feeling, as though I were

in a tunnel and danger was thundering toward me like an express train, making me want to put my fists up and defend myself.

My senses were telling me something bad was coming. Not a sixth sense, just the reptile brain noticing things we don't: a shadow where there shouldn't be one, a noise out of place, an expression on a face that doesn't tally with the body language.

Danger!

I stayed very still, because it had happened to me this way before, and I knew it would pass quickly and everything would go back to normal in a few seconds.

"Freedom, you OK?" Java said suddenly. Her voice sounded like a thunderclap, even though really she had one of those small clear voices.

"What?" I knew I'd said it too loud, like I was shouting over background noise. She made a sudden move toward me, and I sprang back to block it.

"Hey, it's cool," she said, spreading her hands to show she meant no harm. "You were tipping your glass over," she explained, and her voice faded to normal as though someone had turned the world's volume control back down.

"Oh, right." I breathed deeply.

She gave me an uncertain look, maybe glad the table was between us. She probably thought I was going to have a seizure or something. "You OK?" she repeated.

I felt around in my mind for some clue about what I'd

just experienced. "Not sure," I said slowly. But I could feel my muscles bunching themselves without my control.

Something was coming.

The door slammed open. The bell nearly shot off its hook as the frame shook.

Two skinheads, followed by Clunk's friend Hoodie, came at me like rabid dogs, and I found myself up against the window with my face pressed against Mrs. Bunn's lacy curtains while the skinheads found every tender spot in my body and thumped it as hard as they could and Hoodie shouted in my ear about Clunk, who he said was dead now and that I killed him.

**‖‖‖ ‖‖‖
‖‖‖ ‖‖‖ ‖‖‖**

"FREAK!"

It's amazing what stands out when you're being beaten to within an inch of your life.

The skinheads had matching spiderweb tattoos on their hands. I had a very close view of the artwork as their fists came at me time and again. The fists were attached to the usual kind of thugs. Behind them was Hoodie, ranting and raving.

And behind him, standing on her counter, was Mrs. Bunn.

"Quiet now, everyone!" she shouted. "Let's shake and make up, there's no need to — oh dear!"

Of course Hoodie took no notice.

I got myself into a position where most of my vulnerable spots were covered and then tried to make myself as small as possible, so that they couldn't do me much damage. But this was still going to smart in the morning.

I willed myself not to fight back. This was neither the place nor the time. Mrs. Bunn deserved better than that.

I'll give Java one thing, she didn't scream. But it was no place for a girl to be, especially one like her; a Gypsy girl would have been smart enough to get out of the way. Then I heard her posh schoolgirl tones over the top of Hoodie's ranting and raving.

"Stop it this instant!"

Like that was going to happen! Next she'd be calling them oafs.

"Shut up, girl, we're taking care of this scum for you."

And the blows rained down on my back and shoulders. I'd got my arms above my head now, as though I was cowering, but in that position I could see Java and make sure she wasn't in any danger. Jesus, the girl hadn't got the sense she was born with. Instead of running, she was clutching her backpack to her chest and staring like she was frozen.

"Three against one! Leave him alone, you bullies!"

Stupid girl! Why didn't she just clear off and let me get on with things? Luckily Hoodie was focused in on me, and wasn't taking any notice of her.

"People seem to think you're something special. I reckon you got lucky last time, didn't ya? Not this time. This time we're gonna seriously take you down . . . trailer trash!"

"Yeah, trailer trash!"

"Right!" Java again.

In between the blows raining down on me from Spider-

147

Man One and Spider-Man Two, and the ranting coming from Hoodie, I saw her run behind the counter and grab one of Mrs. Bunn's spoons from the stove. No one was taking a blind bit of notice of her, except me. I saw her begin to creep up behind Hoodie.

And now I started to sweat.

She was doomed. She was going to do one of those girlie hits. And then Hoodie would turn, and I didn't think he was the sort to be worried about hitting a girl.

"Wrong," I said, trying to stand, hands up protecting my head, trying to deflect their attention from Java. "Trailer trash live in trailers because they can't afford houses, so they act like their lives stink. Whereas we live in trailers because we know we're blessed." I looked at Hoodie and the Spider-Men, who'd stopped for a moment to sneer at me. "Same trailer, see, but a different way of thinking."

"So?" said Hoodie. "You're still a murderer."

I sucked in a huge breath through my teeth, then let it out in a long hiss. *Fffsssss!*

Hoodie grabbed a sweeping brush and brought it crashing down on my shoulders.

"This is for Clunk! You'll never fight anyone ever again when we've finished with you . . . you understand? . . . And you're gonna leave town, or we'll burn all your trailers down. . . ."

Behind him, Mrs. Bunn stood to attention and began singing "Land of Hope and Glory."

I took another big breath. Building up the pressure.

I felt the blood starting to rush to my head, to my hands, to my feet.

I tensed and untensed my muscles as I crouched in my corner, the blows raining down.

My lungs were at the bursting point. The blood sang through my veins.

"Clunk's dead, Pikey, do you hear me? Dead! Not much of a fighter now, are you?"

I was a coiled spring.

Time to jive. And jiving means never being where they think you are, it means bouncing off walls and sliding across floors. It meant I was going to move so fast that I'd confuse my enemy, and then I wouldn't have to throw a single punch or frighten Mrs. Bunn any more than she was already. I was ashamed enough that the poor old lady'd had to see this in her café.

So as soon as Java tapped Hoodie around the head with the spoon, I exploded into action.

"What the –?"

I went upward, used the wall as a springboard, and somersaulted over their heads, which was a bit of pure showing-off movie action and would have caused old Hercules to shake his head and curse me for being a jackass. Spider-Men One and Two ran into each other in confusion. There was a loud crack as their heads connected.

"Get 'im!"

Hoodie was still screaming, so I grabbed the brush off him and tripped him, leaped onto a table, and knocked Spider-Men One and Two down again just as they were staggering to their feet. There was a muffled thump as they hit the floor. They were fine when they thought I was cowering in the corner, but now they were lost. It wasn't lack of training, but too much. They go to gyms and hit punching bags over and over again, and they do routines and they spar. But that's not fighting. Hit a punching bag and it doesn't hit you back. Hit a real person and all hell breaks loose.

I think it's fair to say that old Hercules never saw a gym in his life. He had only one rule: Hit hard and keep them coming, no matter what.

But I didn't want to hit hard; I didn't want to hit at all in front of Mrs. Bunn. So I ran up the back wall and bounced off the counter and just kept moving. I swear I never touched the floor again after that.

Round and round I went, scattering poor Mrs. Bunn's plates and cakes, using the ice-cream freezer to leap halfway across the café to trip Spider-Man Two just as he staggered to his feet again. And I didn't even have to worry about Hoodie, because he was on his knees and crying, even though Java had hit him as though she were tapping the top of a boiled egg. Really crying, clutching his eyes and blubbing.

But the fun was only just beginning, and I had

Spider-Man One coming at me from the front and Spider-Man Two, who was still on the floor, trying to grab my legs and trip me. Which is why Mrs. Bunn's nice wooden tables and chairs got in on the action. All I'm admitting here is that they couldn't have been very strong in the first place. My Uncle Shady could have got her some that would last through several pub brawls, for a very reasonable price. These things splintered like matchwood as I sprang around the café, not even sprinting now because there was no way they could catch me again. The vases of flowers went flying and the curtains were torn down and the stand holding the cakes went over backward, and Mrs. Bunn had got hold of a rolling pin and was lashing out in every direction.

Blue moon of Kentucky, keep on shinin'...

You notice things during a fight. Odd sounds. Flash frames. A stupid cowboy song floating in through the café door. I saw Java dancing back out of our way, still carrying the serving spoon. It looked like it was tipped with blood, or maybe I'd started hallucinating, because jiving takes it out of you very quickly.

Shine on the one that's gone and left me blue...

Another flash frame, and I glimpsed someone in blue coming through the door. And another, and another.

Police.

Blue moon of Kentucky, keep on shinin'...

And out on the curb, three police cars. And country-and-western music wailing from a big black car.

Shine on the one that's gone and left me blue ...

Another flash frame, a giant coming through the door at speed. Wren.

Next thing I know I'm spread-eagled against the wall of the café with my arm twisted up my back, and three cops were making sure I couldn't move a muscle. There were cops all over the Spider-Men and Hoodie, too.

"Ah, and Miss Sparrow as well," said Wren, taking off his cowboy hat and sprawling himself down in a chair, stretching his back like tall people do. "The girl who stole from her father's company, and here she is wielding a weapon! Tipped with blood?"

Java was still holding her spoon. I hadn't been hallucinating; it *was* tipped with crimson.

"F-f-fresh . . . chili . . . s-s-sauce . . . in his eyes," she stammered, her teeth chattering.

Well, that explained Hoodie's tears, and it had possibly allowed me to get the better of the other two while he was on his knees crying. She dropped the spoon and began bear-hugging herself again, gazing wildly around at the destroyed café and slowly backing toward the door. "You know me?" she said to Wren.

"I heard about your brother's disappearance and I looked into it for a while," he said.

So Johnny Sparrow is *in the Bear Pit*, I thought. But I wondered where this left Java. Was Wren going to arrest the girl and get her off my back?

It turned out that as soon as Wren's attention was diverted to a Spider-Man screaming that his arm was broken, Java turned and fled. Wren let her go; I think he'd got enough to deal with here.

"I never started it! I didn't throw one punch, they kept running into each other!" I said through gritted teeth. The cops still had me in an armlock, and they weren't being gentle. "Tell them to let go."

He signaled to the cops, and not a moment too soon. The café was beginning to dance around before my eyes, and my legs had turned to rubber. Hercules would have been ashamed of me.

I turned and leaned my back against the wall, using it as a prop. Wren tipped his chair back onto two legs and looked at me, his head to one side, his eyes narrowed, his jaw tense. "What the hell happened?" he said.

"Clunk's dead."

Behind him, Mrs. Bunn began weeping at the state of her café. Wren quickly nodded to one of the cops to sort her out. Overhead I heard a few stumbling footsteps. We'd woken her angel, presumably.

"I know. They switched off the life support an hour ago." He rested the cowboy hat on his knee and lit a cigar, but without taking his eyes off me.

There was a scuffle near the door and I saw Hoodie

being handcuffed and escorted out by a bunch of cops.

"Murderer," he shouted at me as he went out. "It's him you should be arresting, not me!" He struggled half out of their hold and threw himself toward me. "Don't listen to what he says, he's a killer!"

"For Christ's sake, Bigley, get them outta here!" said Wren to one of the cops. But I'd seen the look on a couple of the cops' faces when Hoodie had shouted. They agreed with him. They thought I was a killer. Like the spray paint on the trailers, it was a stain that was going to stay with me forever. I turned to Wren.

"The deal's off, I'm not working for you." The wall between me and the blood money hadn't just lost a brick; with Clunk's death it had been razed to the ground.

"We'll see," was all Wren said. But he watched me like a hawk.

I nodded toward the other cops. "See that lot? They think I killed Clunk. Maybe *you* think I killed him." Wren shook his head, but I ignored him. "No matter what I do, no one is going to believe me. There's no use trying to be good."

Wren touched my arm. "You're wrong."

"No, listen." I brushed his hand away and took a few gasping breaths. My stomach felt hollow. "If I help you, the police'll still move us on." I pointed toward the two Spider-Men, who had their hands in restraints and were being led into the back of a police van. "Those skinheads and Hoodie, they'll be out in a couple of days. But we'll be moved on. The cops'll come back and move us into the next county, make us someone else's problem." My head was swimming now. I really needed to get some food. Thai'd be good. Or sugar. Dear Lord, sugar'd be good.

"So what are you saying? That you're just going to move on and forget about your mission?" Wren had never taken his eyes off me, but as the cops began to move out he still managed to signal to a few of them to stay put. They obeyed him as readily as Darcus's men obeyed Darcus.

"I'm going to join the Bear Pit," I said bitterly. "But not to help you. To buy my sister the land, and then you lot can never move us again." Wren shook his head slowly, like he thought I was just ranting, all hyped up after a brawl, talking big. I'd show him. "I'm joining them, Wren. I'm not doing it for you, I'm really joining them."

He ran a hand across his eyes, then through his hair, and put the hat back on. Jeez, who did he think he was — a sheriff from the Wild West? Maybe all the girls in his life thought he looked like a swell guy in it. "I can't let you do that, Smith. I've lost one man to Darcus already. Gabby was our best —"

"Who?" I said sharply.

"Gabriel, our undercover man —"

"The cop who went in and never came back out?" I interrupted, because something, *something* in my mind was trying to get through the low blood sugar and attract my attention, trying to make a connection to something else, but I couldn't think straight, couldn't even stand straight, so I let it go.

"I'm not losing someone else to Darcus," Wren finished.

He fished in his pocket and took out a packet of pills. "Here," he said, handing me one. "Superstrength ibuprofen. You look like you could do with an anti-inflammatory or you'll seize up."

I swallowed it in one gulp. He was right. After the beating I'd taken, my muscles would be stiffening up pretty soon. And I had the feeling that in the near future I was going to have to move very, very fast.

"You're not losing me, I'm going of my own free will." I took some deep breaths to steady myself. "I don't care if it takes a year, I'll earn myself the money fighting, because that's what I am. I'm not a hero, I'm a fighting machine. And I'll get us the land and then no one will ever evict us again."

The gold tooth gleamed for a split second, but there was no humor in Wren's smile. "You could be dead in a year."

Now it was my turn to smile cynically. "I'll live. Fighting's what I do."

Did I mention that usually people keep eye contact for only a few seconds at a time? Wren hadn't looked away from me since he'd stopped the fight. Now I couldn't turn away from him. I wanted to, I felt like he was looking right inside me, and I don't allow anyone to do that. Even I don't delve into my soul very often.

"I can't let you do it, Freedom," he said, chewing on the end of his cigar. "Darcus uses performance enhancers and controls his fighters' minds. No one leaves the Bear Pit, and without your help we can't get in and shut it down."

Still we locked eyes.

"I'll risk it. I won't have to take his steroids, because I can fight without them. And he won't control my mind, because he won't need to. I'll fight for him, earn my fortune, and then be gone."

Wren shook his head at me. "You have no idea what you'd be getting yourself into. Can't let you do it, Freedom."

"Tough."

There was a movement by the door, like quicksilver. Two of the cops moved forward, but they were too slow.

"Fwed!"

A little face suddenly peered up at me, and a pair of tiny hands grabbed on to me with surprising strength. "Fwed, you fought the bad guys! You were a deadeye knight, I seen you!" I gave her a hug and held her like I'd never let go, but it was a lie. I'd be gone shortly.

I glanced out the window. There were police cars over by the trailers as well.

"Fred! Baby boy!" Crystal's face crumpled as she ran up to me. "We're moving. Now!" She pushed herself between me and Wren, giving him a contemptuous look and possibly a Smith elbow to the ribs, because his face twitched for a split second and he bent to one side.

"The gavvers say that skinhead died! They keep talking about you being this champion fighter, well known for being good with your fists, like it's all your fault." Crystal flung back her long dark hair, her eyes glittering. "I says to them, yeah, in defense of himself or his family or the little girls, never unprovoked." Her eyes changed from glittering to tear-filled. She wiped a hand angrily across them. "They say they know different. So I told them to get lost. I told them to give us an hour and we'd be long gone! Come on, Fred boy, let's go and pack!" She pushed by Wren again – stamped by him – and he wisely got his feet out of her way this time. He'd seen her spike heels.

"You go," I said quietly. "I've got stuff to do here. I'll meet up with you later."

That stopped her dead in her tracks. She stopped pulling at my sleeve and dropped Whitney Jade's hand. Somehow she knew straightaway what I meant. She knew I would never meet up with her. She wiped more tears away from her face, angrily, and then stared at me. "What, baby boy?"

I looked down. Body language again. I couldn't meet her eyes. It seemed like the whole world had gone silent. Except for that stupid country-and-western music tinkling away in the background.

"We've lost you, haven't we, Fred?" she said bitterly. "What am I going to tell Mammy?"

I didn't say anything. She stared at me for a few moments more, and then all the anger suddenly went out of her, which was worse. I'm OK with Crystal when she's blazing away, but when she goes sad I can't stand it. I just stood there, leaning against the wall in the wrecked café, my face like thunder. It must have looked like I didn't care, but I was destroyed inside.

"We lost you a long time ago, didn't we?" Crystal whispered.

I nodded. They shouldn't have bred me as a fighter.

"What's to become of you?" she said sadly.

Then Whitney Jade started crying and I picked her up and told her to stop being silly, and that I was a Jedi Knight and no one would ever catch me.

Wren must have given them the signal at that point, while I was off guard.

There was a sudden flurry of movement. Crystal screamed. A big hand grabbed my shoulder, and someone snatched Whitney Jade out of my arms.

"Sorry, Freedom, I'd rather have you arrested than loose in that place. I can't let you do it," said Wren, stepping back so that two of the biggest cops could spin me around, slam me against the wall again, and get a police hold on me. The way they held me made it clear they weren't going to let go in a hurry.

There was only one way I was going to get out of this.

TTH TTH II
TTH TTH TTH

Time stood still; no one moved. I waited for my chance.

Whitney Jade, held hostage in the arms of a cop, finished inhaling about a million gallons of air, and screamed.

That was the chance.

It was a scream from the dawn of time. It would have stopped a saber-toothed tiger in its tracks, so the police never stood a chance.

"Hold him!" warned Wren, but he was too far away.

For a millisecond, everyone within twenty feet of her turned toward the terrible sound. It's like when there's a fox near your trailer and it catches a rabbit and the rabbit screams, and you wake with your heart thumping and your spine turned to jelly, and all you want to do is stop the terrible noise. That's how Whitney Jade screams, like she's being tortured to death. The sound jarred at our very souls, and everyone had the same panicked thought: Find the noise and stop it.

Except me, I'm used to her bawling. So when I felt the cops turn ever so slightly, loosening their grip on me ever so slightly as well, with just a tiny part of their brains thinking, *Oh my God, we've injured a child, there'll be lawsuits about this and we'll be to blame*, I went downward first, to break their hold on my arm, so that when I then went upward like a rocket I wouldn't dislocate my shoulder. That was the theory, anyway. It hurt like hell, but I was free at least.

"Get him!" barked Wren, but I was over the scattered tables, swerving around his long reach and out of the café before Whitney Jade had even finished her first lungful.

"Freedom! You idiot, stop!" he yelled after me. And I saw him come barreling out of the café, but he was too late.

I was already on the wall of the pub just as the cops got off their starting blocks and began either running after me or getting back in the cars ready to drive around and cut me off from the next street. As if. And just to show how unconcerned I was about them ever catching me, I tightroped along a narrow bit of wall, did a forward flip, and blew a kiss to Whitney Jade.

Then I moved fast. I knew exactly what I was going to do. I went across town using roofs and back alleys. I stopped only once, in the shopping center. When I got to the cathedral I found myself a space next to a gargoyle and curled myself up into a similar position, my arms hugging my knees. Then I ate my take-out. Tom Yum soup, extra hot, Poh Piah, and a bag of Thorntons assorted chocolates. I was starving, and when I'd eaten everything except half the bag of chocolates, I started to feel the shakes leave my legs and I started to think clearly, too.

Wren, stuff him. My family? I was just a burden to them. I was no use to anyone except one person.

Darcus Knight.

I'd send my family the money when I'd made enough, and then I'd be free.

The only thing I was good at was fighting, so that's what I'd do. Then the only people I'd hurt would be me and those like me.

Which just left Java.

●　◀　◀

Way past midnight I made my way back to the café. I kept to the roofs and came in over the top of Mrs. Bunn's. At first I thought Java had packed up her sleeping bag and gone home. But then I noticed the door to Mrs. Bunn's cellar was ajar, and I thought I heard movements inside. So I went in and said, "Anyone at home?" in case it was Mrs. Bunn herself. But, wouldn't you know it, there was Java, lying fast asleep on a bed she'd made from flattened cardboard boxes and some old blankets, squashed in between the sacks of spuds, racks of tins and bottles, and bags of flour that filled the cellar.

It must have been the feral tabby cat making the noise, because it shot out of the cellar when it saw me.

It couldn't have been Java, because when I shook her she shrugged me off and kept on sleeping, like she'd been asleep for hours. I wished I could have lain down and closed my eyes as well. Last night hadn't exactly been restful.

As I bent down to her, something rolled from her pocket. It was her bottle of Buttercup syrup. I picked it up and threw it into the trash can nearby, and her tin of roll-ups for good measure. I hated seeing people relying on stuff like that. Then I shook her again, but all that happened was she ended up leaning against me.

"Nice," she said.

My heart pounded but I ignored it. My path was set now.

"That was some fight in the café," she said suddenly, looking up at me. "You're dangerous!"

"I'm the end product of a long line of fighters and scrappers, love," I said. "I'm a fighter distilled. I'm a violent thug. I'm a freak." I gave a short laugh. "And I've got the webbed toes to prove it."

It was dark and lonely down in the cellar. She should have been scared. She should have flinched away. But this is *my* life I'm describing here, and it was never going to happen. So she just shook her head, as you might at a child who's telling really big whoppers, then pinned me with her gaze.

"Except you never threw one punch back there, even when they were hitting you really hard," she said. "My mum told me that you're not bad." She smiled her sleepy smile at me. "She's wondering where you're going now."

She was talking in her sleep, so I said, "Into Darcus's fight. I'm finished with this life, I just keep messing everything up. If I see your brother I'll tell him you're worried. But don't expect anything more. We all have our own lives to lead. You should get back to yours and forget about Johnny."

She didn't answer.

"Hey, Java," I whispered.

"Hey, Freedom," she said sleepily.

"It's been nice knowing you," I said quietly. I squatted beside her for a minute. "In a different life, we could have got together, maybe. But I've got this theory that there's two worlds, see. 'World A' and 'World B.'"

"Sounds nice," she murmured, leaning her head on my shoulder and sighing. "Tell me 'bout it."

"'World B' is the edgy one, where there's no safety net and you live on the fringes and survive on your wits."

"Mmmm. I like it!" She was half asleep; she didn't know what she was saying or what I was saying. Thank goodness.

"It's like a knickerbocker glory, fun and disasters all thrown together, and happiness is a great big belly laugh and riding bareback at fairs and not caring about anything like exams and careers but just living life as it comes."

"Kushti!" she said, her eyes closed, head still against me.

I waited till she was asleep again. "Problem is, 'World A' holds all the power," I said, and left her there.

Then I rang the police anonymously and told them there was a fifteen-year-old runaway in the cellar behind the café, and that she was a thief. That should keep her out of the way until her father could come and collect her, and his money.

I waited till I heard the sirens, gave her one last lost look, and walked out of her life.

◆ ◆ ◆

"Yo, Wren here ... Hi, Snow ... No, everything's fine. ... You heard Freedom had run off? Bad news sure travels fast, but in this case it's wrong, he's still working for us ... he's still on the case. ... No, I'm not kidding. ... He may not know *he's still working for us, but he is. ... I know his whereabouts down to the last inch ... you could say I'm like his nanny. ... No, Snow, I'm not going to explain myself any more, you'll just have to figure it out for yourself. ... Catch you later. ..."*

⫴⫴⫴ ⫴⫴⫴ ⦀
⫴⫴⫴ ⫴⫴⫴ ⫴⫴⫴

The cage slammed to a halt at the bottom of the long shaft, its ancient brakes squealing. A bell pinged and a little sign saying PRACTICE ARENA began flashing. I heaved the door open and stepped out.

Danger!

I crouched. A shadow flickered far away and was gone. I glanced around.

Beneath the grim exterior of the building a whole new world spread before me, a subterranean labyrinth of half-light and endless tunnels. The goon upstairs had told me it was so vast that it'd been used during the last war as an air-raid shelter for thousands of people. And, before that, for storing and making chemicals.

The goon had also given me rough directions. The elevator came out onto a massive tunnel that enclosed the whole complex like a ring road. Smaller tunnels ran off it, like spokes from the rim of a wheel. They met in the center at a huge practice arena. I'd been told to report there, but for now I stayed against the elevator and stared into the gloom.

The air was hot and heavy, like the breath of some

beast panting in my face. Everything was gray, except for some nightmare plants that had sprouted in the dark. Fungus had gathered in corners and crevices, some of it black, some dark green, linked by patches of white mold like dead skin, glistening in the twilight and smelling of graveyards. Farther up the walls, mosses and vines two feet long trailed like zombies' hair from the bottoms of the huge fans that were sluggishly moving the air throughout the tunnels.

There it was again! *Danger!*

I didn't like being underground any more than I liked boxing rings or any sort of prison, but that wasn't what was bothering my reptile senses and making my hackles rise.

I kept my back against the elevator doors. They were vibrating, like a ticking heart.

Evil. There's evil down here.

And my human brain wanted to say, *Well, what did you expect from an illegal bare-knuckle fighting operation, a choir of angels to greet you?* But even then I knew it was more than the aura of violence that fights give off. I was used to fights. This was something else. Something ancient, something primeval was stalking the dank tunnels and caverns of Darcus's submerged world. Something big. Something very different from the tiny little hand that had appeared from the side of the elevator shaft and was trying to sneak into my pocket.

I grabbed and pulled. Ant, the little kid who lived

under the boxing ring, shot out and dangled in front of me, like a rabbit pulled from a magician's hat. Then, slowly and uncertainly, like animals used to being whipped, five or six more kids crept out from beneath the elevator shaft. These were bigger kids, maybe ten years old, but just as dirty and bedraggled, and all dressed like miniature terrorists. They gathered around me, eyes bright in the darkness.

"Did you bring any candy?" said Ant.

I had, but going by the state of the teeth I was seeing, I shouldn't have. I got out the bag of Thorntons chocolates. "Here, have one each. They're the nectar of the gods, so don't wolf them." I put the bag back in my pocket. Several pairs of eyes watched it go.

I let Ant have a few sucks on his chocolate, and then grabbed his hand and made him look at me. "You've just given me the holy horrors," I said sternly. "You could've got squashed in that elevator shaft."

He looked at me with his puppy-dog eyes. "We was hiding from the monster."

So that would be the evil I felt. One of the fighters gone crazy, maybe, and lurking in the tunnels, frightening the little kids. "What does your monster do?"

Ant's lip curled, and a brown dribble escaped and went straight down his front. It didn't improve the color of his clothes, or his stickiness. "If he catches you, he takes you away and doesn't bring you back."

Ice ran down my spine despite the hot air blowing

down the tunnels. At the far end of one of them, a shadow flickered for a moment again and was gone. "I might just go and have a look for your monster, see him for myself," I said grimly, and Ant looked at me like I was his knight in shining armor. I tried to let go of his hand, but it seemed we were stuck together.

"Are you from outside?" said one of the bigger ones.

"Yeah."

Go down in the cage and the Tunnel Rats will show you the way, I'd been told at reception. These were the "Rats," I guessed.

"What's it like outside? It's deadly, isn't it?" he continued. "People kill you in the streets, they cut your head off and steal your money."

"No, they don't," I said. Not that often, anyway. Ant tugged at my hand.

"And there's witches out there," he said in his micro-voice. "In the big world."

"Who told you that?" I said.

"They dance around in robes and cast spells. Darcus told us."

"Not that I've ever seen." But it was a useful thing to tell little kids, if you didn't want them to stray. It was like a preacher telling believers that the devil would get them unless they followed what he said. But I was puzzled. Where had all these kids come from?

"What's your other name, Ant?" I said.

He shrugged. "Ant?" Like he wasn't even sure about his first name, never mind his last.

"Short for Anthony?" I said.

Another boy said, "No, mister, Ant's not his name, it's what he is. An ant." He pointed at his friends. "The fighting men call us Rats, but he's too little to be a Rat, so he's an ant."

Jeez, that made me feel bad. I know I'd made my decision to join the fight, but I didn't have to like everything about it. And I didn't like this at all.

"How did you get here? Where do you come from? Where's your mammies and daddies?" I asked. But there were shrugs all around.

"We're just here," said Ant.

"You know what?" said another, in a spiteful voice like kids use to the teacher when they're telling on another kid.

"What?"

He pointed at Ant. "He's got a picture of his mummy." The other Rats sniggered. Ant bunched his tiny fists.

"Show me," I said. The little boy rummaged in a foul greasy pocket in his combat pants, and took out some creased and tattered photos wrapped in an old bandanna.

The top one was a picture of Kylie Minogue cut out of a mag.

"Is that your mammy?" Ant nodded and gave a tiny smile about a micron wide. The other kids collapsed with laughter. Dear God, my heart ached for him, standing there with his picture of Kylie Minogue, but then something more sinister caught my eye.

"Where did you get these from?" I said quietly.

"He's got lots of pictures," said one of them. "He steals them. Darcus'll kill him if he ever finds out."

"Give us a squint," I said, my heart beating a tattoo. Ant handed them over. Underneath Kylie was a black-and-white photo. This one hadn't been cut out of a mag. It had been taken with a telephoto lens by the look of it, because everything had that crowded-together look. It was a picture of a horse fair, and I knew which one. I'd been there every May since I'd been born.

Stow Fair, where Gypsy men go to sell their horses and jaw with their pals. And where the women buy their jewelry, and the girls wear their best clothes and go around looking at the boys, who ride bareback on painted horses, showing their paces to buyers. That's what this old creased photo showed. A crowd of traveling people enjoying their fair, just as they had for hundreds of years. And in the foreground was a young Gypsy lad, spiky-haired and dark-eyed, riding bareback with just a bridle, riding like the wind so that the background was a speed blur, showing off the paces of his black-and-white horse, its long mane and tail floating out behind in the wind.

"Why did you steal this picture?" I asked slowly.

Ant looked at me solemnly. "I liked the horsey."

So had I. It was my horse, and the freckly squinting kid on the back was me at seven years old. The horse, my daddy's favorite, was a stallion named Destiny. We sold him for a tidy sum that year.

I bent down so that I was level with Ant. "Where'd you get this?"

His eyes grew round and scared.

"No, it's OK," I said quickly. "I'm not mad or nothing, I'm not going to tell, swear to God."

"Darcus," he whispered.

We've been watching you a long time, Wren had said, *and so has Darcus.*

I straightened up. I now had three things to do: Tell my reptile senses to shut up whining and take a break. Get my bearings. And then find Darcus. I wanted a word.

I started walking down one of the tunnels. The kids traipsed along with me, Ant still holding my hand.

"Look, I can gallop like a pony," he said, doing a little giddyup run, but his legs were so small that he had to take about three or four little gallops for every one of my strides. It was sad, that's what it was. My mammy would have gone crazy to see a little kid living down here. We're outdoors people; even the little babies in our family can be seen in their buggies with their hair blowing in the wind. It's the best way to be. No one thrives underground.

We walked some more. The tunnel was one of the main spokes heading straight toward the hub. But there were others we passed that led off at right angles and disappeared into the blackness, or showed glimpses of dimly lit rooms full of equipment or bunks. These side tunnels looked ancient, their ceilings low and some of them half collapsed. But a couple of times we had to take a detour into them because even our tunnel had a few blockages caused by roof falls. I filed every turn and step in my mind, just as I did when the Smiths went traveling. When we were on the move we never had to look at a map, we kept the route in our heads. I was a long way from the elevator now, and there weren't many markers underground for my Gypsy compass to lock on to; I was having to pay real attention. Sometime I might want to leave in a hurry.

After a few more minutes the tunnel widened out and began to fill with men converging from every direction. No one took any notice of us.

A fighter stamped by me and pushed me against the wall. The vibration I'd felt earlier was still there. "Why is this place beating?" I said.

"Don't lean against the wall, or you'll never get out!" said Ant, pulling at my hand.

One of the older Rats cuffed him around the ear. "Shut it! Don't tell him!"

"But he bringed us candy," said Ant. "He's going to get the monster, and I'm going to be his boy."

"We said we'd never tell," hissed the other kid. "Or else." He made a slitting motion across his throat.

"But he's good!" Ant pulled me down so he could whisper. "We have a plan, don't tell, will you?" I shook my head. "One day the bigger boys say they'll break out and they're going to take us with them. But when we lean against the walls and the heartbeat gets us, we forget about the plan . . . it makes our brains go dreamy."

"Some of the big boys want to get out, too?" I said. Ant cupped his sticky hands around my ear.

"Shh, don't tell, but they don't take their pills, they hide them, and then they pretend to fight. Darcus and Rachel don't know." He giggled.

"And the heartbeat in the walls makes you forget your plan?"

"Watch!" Ant leaned against the wall with his eyes shut. His little face went blank. The other Rats lay themselves against the wall, too.

"We love the heartbeat!" said one of them, and his eyes became dreamy.

I put my hand on the vibrating wall and my thoughts began to scatter. I pulled my hand back quickly. The heartbeat in the walls was putting our brain waves into alpha mode. This was something else my old boxing coach'd told me. How there were gyms where the coaches used brainwashing to get their fighters to believe they'd win every time. They did it like the stage hypnotists. Got their boxers thinking in alpha by using special sounds. Then told 'em they were the greatest, that they were invincible. Coach said it worked. But it was still brainwashing. And Darcus's version was much worse, because there seemed to be no escape from it.

"When are they going to put the escape plan into operation?" I asked.

Ant looked downcast. "The big boys always say, be patient, stay quiet, it'll happen tomorrow. But then when tomorrow comes, it's not tomorrow anymore, it's today. And we don't do the plan."

"Manhunt starting . . . this is a call for Clan Eagle, Clan Fortune – to the practice arena, please," said a loudspeaker above our heads. "Let's fight the glorious fight, the fight that never ends."

It was Darcus's voice, but not the wrecked and whispery one I'd heard before. His voice now was rich, rolling, and hypnotic, like the voice of a preacher man. Either the frail voice was a put-on, or he had a powerful booster on his mike.

Two groups of men, some in leather, some in war paint, some looking like they'd just stepped off a battlefield during the Second World War, looked up when they heard Darcus's voice. Even though they looked tired, their eyes began to gleam, and they gripped their weapons, straightened their shoulders, and trooped off.

"Clan Fortune is a man down, so can we have backup, please?" continued the loudspeaker.

A warrior in black leaped down from a bench and followed them out.

All around me fighters were collecting weapons, warming up their muscles, shouting to one another, working themselves up into a fury. The stone walls were medieval, but the sound system was twenty-first century.

"Call for Clan Half-Life stand ready, that's all for now. Everyone into positions for the Bear Pit. All fighters report to your refs when your name is called. . . ."

We flattened ourselves against the damp wall as the fighters pushed past.

Skirting around us in the gloom were soldiers, gladiators, Vikings, Zulus, samurai, and zombies. Some were tattered and torn, some had faces blackened or covered in war paint. Plenty had bruises and cuts, with rags tied around wounds, like they'd been through a war. Other fighters looked like preacher men with rabid eyes full of hellfire and damnation; some were robotic, psyched out, like the jackals, who seemed to be everywhere, stalking the corridors, always in a group, never smiling; some just looked like the walking dead, all hope gone.

The Tunnel Rats began to slip away. It seemed that they all had a certain fighter they worked for – except for Ant. His hand stayed stuck to mine, thanks mainly to the chocolates.

No one spoke to me, but I got plenty of black looks. It was like school all over again. Me the new kid – and as a traveler I was always the new kid – trying to decide whether to be quiet and blend in or to slug it out right from the word go and show them I wasn't to be messed with.

And even here, as the fighters pushed past, I still felt that something terrible was close behind me – "Monster!" whispered Ant, looking fearfully over his shoulder – and every so often we heard the small telltale noises of something lurking in the side tunnels, and the occasional scent of a savage creature blown to us by the slowly whirring fans.

"Where are the other boys going?"

"To help the fighters, that's our jobs," he continued. "We bring them drinks and change their weapons. The other boys've all got fighters. I ain't got anyone, I'm too little. Can I be your boy?"

"Yep," I said. I fished out another chocolate. "Let's seal the deal with a candy."

God help the poor little kid's teeth, but he looked like he was in heaven.

Most of the fighters had headed off along the tunnel to the practice arena. There was a bit of a bottleneck as they shoved and pushed each other, all hyped up and ready to fight. I kept back, away from them.

"Newbie?" said a bright voice from behind me. It was the sort of voice that might deliver the right answer in a math class. A voice at odds with the growls I'd heard so far. A hand was thrust in my direction.

"Hi, do you need some help?"

Johnny Sparrow.

₩₩ ₩₩ ||||
₩₩ ₩₩ ₩₩

"**I**'ve got to report to Darcus," I said.

Jeez, he looked like his sister, more so than the missing posters had shown. The same pointed face, like a Japanese cartoon, the same eyes. Except Java didn't have quite so much in the way of split lips, bruised cheekbones, or the hideous black bruise over the ribs as though a horse had kicked him. All in all, he looked a mess.

"I'll show you," he said.

"No, *I'll* show you!" said Ant quickly. "I'm your boy."

I bent down and said, "The first rule of being my boy is to be quiet." Which meant I had to give him another chocolate because his lip trembled and he looked at me with his puppy-dog eyes.

Then I shook Johnny's thin hand. I swear the Sparrow children must have been fed on birdseed when they were babies. He was skinny all over, but you could tell he'd been well trained at one time.

He swayed about a bit as a group of fighters pushed by. Even Ant had to help steady him. "You OK?" I said.

"Yeah," he said, trying not to move his cut lip too much. "First time up there in the Bear Pit a few hours ago."

He pointed to the ceiling. That figured. There had been two buttons on the elevator, the bottom one stopping at the practice arena, and the top one labeled THE BEAR PIT.

"What's it like?" I said.

"Glorious," said Johnny, but a second later his face twisted in agony as a fighter elbowed him in the ribs to get him to shift out of the way. "Actually, it hurts . . . like . . . hell," he grunted, but then he noticed some fighters nearby watching him, and laughed suddenly. "No. Really, it's glorious, man. You wait till *you* get a chance to see the Bear Pit." He looked around, his eyes alight again, and spread his arms wide. "The glorious fight."

"You don't look so good," I said. That was a bad bruise on his ribs; I reckoned he'd been kicked by someone who hadn't been messing around.

"Just need a rest," he said, limping on down the rim tunnel and beckoning me after him. He was right; with his injuries, he needed sleep so that his muscle tissues could recover.

"Go and get one, then," I said. "Point out the way, and I'll take it from there."

Johnny shook his head. "Darcus is in the practice arena. Got to go there myself, anyway. You have to be dead not to fight here." He leaned on my arm for a moment and looked at the fighters pushing and shoving in the tunnel ahead of us. He winced. "I know a shortcut, so we don't have to fight our way through. We're not supposed to use the oldest tunnels because they might collapse, but I'm just so tired at the moment . . ."

"Don't go in that one!" said Ant when he saw where Johnny was heading. He grabbed me with his sticky hands, but I pulled him along. "The monster will get us!" he howled.

"I thought you were my boy," I said. "You've got to do what I say."

Ant thought about this, then nodded and walked even closer to my side.

We turned out of the main tunnel into an ancient narrow one, with a low ceiling. I put my hand on the stone wall. The heartbeat was still there. If it was what I suspected, then it would be everywhere, vibrating through every surface of the labyrinth.

"Is it still morning?" I asked Johnny. We were so far belowground that hours could have passed since I'd walked up to the studios, put my finger on the bell, and kept it there.

Johnny shrugged as best he could with his bruised ribs. "It doesn't matter down here," he said. "Eat and sleep when you want. We're on the go 24/7." He started to give a grin, then winced and changed his mind. "Just make sure you get to the Bear Pit for your fights."

"How will I know?"

He nodded back toward the main rim tunnel. "Loudspeakers. You'll be told when you've a fight coming up, and then you wait and listen for your name." He narrowed his eyes. "If you miss a fight, you'll know soon enough."

Ant squeezed my hand. "They hurt you."

"Discipline, that's what Darcus believes in," said Johnny. "Don't mess around, that's my warning."

We'll see about that, I thought. I had a few questions to put to Darcus before I got myself beaten up like Johnny here.

We walked on. Ant was having a jolly time skipping in and out of a line of winking LED lights that were linked down the side of the tunnel like cheap Christmas tree lights. Every so often the wire connecting them ran into a metal box bolted to the stone wall.

"Perimeter alarms," said Johnny when I stopped to get a closer look. "They run around the outside of the complex, to warn of a police raid. This place has never been breached!"

"Cool," I said, and we kept on.

Except I was sweating a bit now, because Johnny had been misinformed. Guns weren't the only thing I knew on sight. I knew a fair bit about explosives, too, my Uncle Shady once being employed in the demolition trade, and I was pretty sure those Christmas tree lights weren't anything to do with a perimeter alarm system. If anyone broke in, those Christmas tree lights would trigger a whole circuit of small but powerful incendiary devices and bring those stone ceilings crashing down in a split second.

The whole complex was booby-trapped and primed to blow up if discovered. And someone was holding the remote control. Darcus, I guessed.

It didn't do much to make me feel better about this place. If Darcus got wind of a police raid, would he worry whether all his fighters were out of the place before he pressed the button? Wren hadn't been joking when he'd said the place was hard to infiltrate.

Johnny glanced ahead. "The trouble with this shortcut is we have to go through an old chemical pool and it's usually half full of water. So you're going to get your feet wet."

I shrugged. After what I'd been through, a little water wasn't going to matter.

"You like it down here?" I asked him as we walked on down the tunnel, stepping over bits of the roof stone that had fallen. "Don't you miss your family and your friends?"

Johnny smiled as best he could with his split lip. His eyes had the look that my Auntie Star got when she became born again. "You're a newbie. You don't understand yet. But you'll see. Nothing else matters but the glorious fight, the fight that never stops." He went to throw his arms wide to show how he loved the place, but he winced and clutched his ribs. He hesitated, like he'd lost the thread of what he was saying. Then he pulled himself together. "It's so simple; I hadn't realized my destiny before. Now I'm prepared to trust Darcus in all things. In this place all my questions are answered, all my doubts soothed. This is home."

"Oh, right," I said. "Good for you."

According to Java, his real home hadn't been up to much. And when no one wants you and you suddenly find someone who does, whether it's God or Darcus Knight, then some people follow without question.

Ahead of us the tunnel opened out and, just as Johnny had said, we now had to cross what looked like an old swimming pool with two feet of water in the bottom. The water was a filthy red, as though it was still poisoned with chemicals.

"Don't like water!" said Ant. I could tell that by the stickiness of him. He grabbed the back of my T-shirt and leaped on my back. He weighed about as much as a flea, but I don't suppose Red Bull, candy, and potato chips were good for solid bone growth.

Johnny put his hand out and stopped me as we got close. "What the –?"

Down in the pool two fighters about my age had found one of the Rats to torment and were beating him up. The kid had got his hands above his head as they rained blows down on him.

Johnny froze. Maybe this sort of thing didn't normally happen and it had knocked his faith in Darcus and the fight. I left him and leaped into the red water, Ant still clinging to my back like a limpet. Whoever the hooded victim was, he was bigger than the rest of the Rats I'd met. And he hadn't gone for the bandanna-and-combats look, but had a hooded top pulled well up over his face and a woolly hat pulled well down underneath. Only a tiny scrap of furious face could be seen.

"Sweet Mercy!" It felt like I'd leaped backward, but I don't know whether I had. This was madness; this could get us all killed.

"It's, uh, just a Tunnel Rat," said Johnny, wading up to me. He sounded in pain. "That's what they call the kids here. They're always getting on someone's nerves. They get a thick ear and run off, that's all." He put a hand on my shoulder to slow me down. "We, um, we have to leave. Come on."

I looked at Johnny. He kept blinking, as though if he did it often enough the scene in front of him would go away.

"It's no Rat," I said, and made for the nearest fighter, heaved him off the hooded figure, and flung him away. He hit the water, went under, and came up retching and coughing.

"Lay off me!" he howled. "Get the outsider!"

The other fighter swung at me, hampered by Ant, who had grabbed on to his leg and was swinging from it, soaking wet, like a terrier with its teeth locked. "Security, get Security!" the fighter yelled.

There was no time for niceties. I tripped him and he went under, like his friend. That stopped the shouting. The red water smelled like bad eggs, so he'd got his mouth closed even before he fell in. Ant bobbed up, and I grabbed him and swung him onto the side of the pool. The first fighter took one look at me, scrabbled to his feet, and scuttled off. I picked up the other one.

He flinched. "Later," he said, wrenching his arm away from me. And then he splashed hastily after his friend. Maybe the jackal with the bleached bangs had warned them to leave the newbie alone.

That just left me and their hooded victim.

I held my hand out to Java, and she took it and stood up.

||||| ||||| |||||
||||| ||||| |||||

"**D**on't say a word," Java said grimly. "It might have worked."

I looked around anxiously. The kid had yelled for Security, so a goon might be on his way.

I grabbed Ant. "I need someone to watch out for Security."

He wiped his nose on his sleeve. "Me. I'll do it!" he said, and skipped off to the far side of the pool and began patrolling up and down, like a little meerkat.

I turned back to Java. "How did you get in?" I said urgently. There were two exits on the far side of the chemical pool. One was brightly lit and looked as if it led to the practice arena. The other was a tiny low tunnel, like you'd see in an old mine, and looked ready to collapse. A sign across the entrance said KEEP OUT: DANGER.

"Down there," said Java. Then she saw Johnny. "Oh God, you're OK!"

He splashed toward us, looking confused.

"Java? I thought it was you – why the hell are you

187

here?" He stopped and clutched his head like it was going to explode. "Why don't you just leave me alone?" he ranted. "Quit following me! Get lost!"

I grabbed Java's arm. "Your brother's not like he was," I said quietly. "He's changed. They give them steroids, he hardly knows what he's saying. I swear he's got a couple of busted ribs, but he's acting like he's fine and just waiting for the next fight."

But Johnny pushed by me and began raving again. "I'm sick of you, Java, you're always trying to tell me what to do! Stop following me!" Java folded her arms and stared at him.

"He doesn't mean it," I muttered.

A big smile flickered across her face. "Yes, he does. That's normal for Johnny. He's not got steroid rage, he always yells at me like that. He's fine." Then she turned on him. "Oh, for heaven's sake, just shut up!" she yelled, then stamped her foot – not a wise move in two feet of filthy red water. It drenched Johnny.

"Don't you ever go off and do something stupid like this again!" She kicked the water at him again. "Or I'm telling Mum!"

The splash of cold water seemed to shock him into silence. He rubbed the water from his face and touched Java's arm like he couldn't believe she was real. "No, I'm dreaming this, you're not really here. This is because I didn't take my pill. . . ." He reached in his pocket and took out a pill.

Ant must've seen because he stopped patrolling and came over. "That's the bad candy!"

"Johnny! Don't take it! Are you crazy?" said Java, grabbing for it. He pulled his hand away.

"It's so we perform better. But I stopped taking mine, I hid them, because I've always thought steroids and performance enhancers are cheating. . . ."

"Yes, they are, so don't take it!"

But he swallowed the pill. "No, they help me! They make me concentrate on the fight. Then I don't think about the outside world."

"You idiot!" said Java.

I stood myself between them, just in case they started fighting. "For heaven's sake, let's just calm down and move back down the tunnel. Security will be on the way."

We got ourselves out of the water and started back the way we came. I was looking for somewhere we could hide.

"Wait," said Java. "Johnny's not keeping up."

"Oh no, oh no," said Ant. "He's gone crazy. He needs the white candy!"

"What?" I said.

"The black candy gives you power and makes you roar and fight," said Ant. "And the white candy makes you nice again and not want to hit everyone!"

I glanced back at Johnny. His eyes had gone dark and distant, and he was clenching and unclenching his fists. The pill he'd taken had begun to work.

"Quick, where can we get this white pill?" I said to Ant.

But it was too late. A goon with a walkie-talkie appeared at the far end of the tunnel and yelled, "Stay right where you are!"

We froze. One second, two seconds, and then Johnny grabbed Java.

"We've got an infiltrator here!" he shouted.

The goon moved forward. Ant gave a squeak and hid behind me.

"Hey, it's cool, we're just messing around!" I shouted. Then I hissed to Johnny, "It's your sister, you lunatic!"

He blinked, and seemed to be trying to focus on her.

"Jav –" he began, then stopped and grimaced like he'd suddenly had a sharp pain in his head. He pulled away from my hand. "No. Uh, no Java," he stammered. "No, uh, sister. No family. This is my family now. I'm home." And he grabbed Java and shoved her roughly toward the goon, who was already muttering into his walkie-talkie. "Infiltrator!" he shouted.

And then he walked away like he didn't know her.

‖‖ ‖‖ ‖‖
‖‖ ‖‖ ‖‖
|

"**S**tay right where you are!" shouted the goon again.

I had about twenty seconds to think up a story.

Java was backed against the wall, gazing after Johnny in horror. "Those pills are evil! Did you see how fast they worked?"

She was rubbing her arms where the fighters had hit her, but she'd got the growly face on again, which probably meant she was planning something.

"We've got to get him out of here," she whispered.

The goon was saying something into the walkie-talkie.

"How did you get away from the police?" I hissed.

She turned on me and gave me a scornful look.

"I was pretending to be asleep, of course," she said, like I was simple or something. "You caught me trying to find the secret passage in Mrs. Bunn's cellar, the one that showed up as the parchmark on the photo. And then you told me to forget about Johnny, so I knew it was up to me to come and look for him myself."

"Didn't do you much good, did it?" I hissed, which got

me a laser-beam stare and a frown. "Look, we'll tell him you're an escaped lunatic or something – and then when you get out of here, stay out, and don't come back."

The frown deepened. "No, I have to get Johnny."

Sweet Mercy, she never listened. "You've seen him. He gave you away. He's not going to leave with you."

"He's only half brainwashed. He was OK until he took the pill. So all I've got to do is stop him –"

"I'll get him."

"No, you need me. I can do the thinking, you can do the fighting."

I was just about to tell her that I could do my own thinking when she fixed me with another laser-beam look and said, "Oh, by the way, I remember everything you said about 'World A' and 'World B.'"

That stopped me in my tracks. I didn't think a jaded Gypsy boy like me could ever turn red, but I did. Thank God it was semidark. If we ever got out of this, I'd have a bit of explaining to do.

At which point Rachel appeared at the end of the tunnel. From behind me came another squeak, and I caught a glimpse of Ant fleeing for the safety of the shadows.

Java and I locked eyes for a split second. "I'm going to start crying," she whispered. "It usually works. You come out with an explanation."

"Do you ever cry for real?" I said.

She blinked. "Not since my mum died. Now make sure your explanation is a good one."

Which gave me about a tenth of a second to think of one. Luckily, living on the edge has given me lots of practice at dreaming up excuses on the spur of the moment.

"There's been a bit of a mistake here," I said, walking toward Rachel with Java trailing behind. "It's the girl who came for the hockey video. She got lost and ended up down here." I gestured to Rachel to move away a little, as though I was going to say something between the two of us, but I made sure my voice carried. "She hasn't a clue what's going on. She thinks this is a film set. And she thinks the boys who roughed her up are Security!"

Right on cue Java burst into tears. She was very good at the pretend tears. I hoped she was fooling Rachel as well as she'd fooled me. Seemed like she was, because Rachel put an arm around her shoulders. I saw Java pull away, like she couldn't bear Rachel anywhere near her.

"There, there, don't cry," Rachel said.

"You gave me the wrong video, and my head teacher sent me back with it," Java sobbed. "A man let me in and then said wait, but he didn't come back, and our headmistress always tells us to be resourceful, and there was an elevator and I thought I'd go and find him, but I got lost, and I don't know how I ended up here, but I did. . . ."

"Shh," said Rachel. "Now come with me. You need to stay upstairs. No one's allowed down here because we're filming at the moment." Rachel steered Java away and smiled at me. "I'll deal with this, Freedom. You can carry on now. Darcus is waiting for you."

I watched until they'd turned the corner. Maybe Darcus *was* waiting for me, but I had other plans.

卌 卌 卌
卌 卌 卌
||

"**N**ot down there, that's where the monster lives! He'll eat you!"

We'd squeezed by the sign that said KEEP OUT: DANGER, that's why Ant was stuck to my leg again, and crying. I was looking for the secret entrance, the one that showed up as the long straight parchmark in the photo on Java's computer. Somewhere in this old condemned tunnel there must be another smaller one. And it must be well hidden because no one else had discovered it.

I pulled out the bag of chocolates. "Shut up and have a candy."

"Yay!" Ant gave a tiny smile. He was learning fast that if he complained, he got another chocolate, but this time it took two to calm him down enough to go near Java's old derelict tunnel. The monster had certainly petrified the kids.

Don't get me wrong, I wasn't thinking of making an escape at that point. I still wanted to fight, I wanted my money. But I had to make sure that Java couldn't risk her life and mine by getting back in, now that Rachel had seen her off the premises.

"See, it's fine," I said as we stepped over the fallen stones and rubble. "Nothing here." But Ant still hid behind me.

I found what I was looking for a long way down the tunnel, where the roof had started to cave in, the walls were crumbling, and the light was just a memory. It was halfway up a stone wall running with green damp.

No one had noticed it because it was covered with a thick tangle of ivy and mosses, hanging down the wall in a huge waterfall of dark green leaves and tangled stems as strong as steel. Behind the greenery there was a small opening at head height, with iron prison bars spaced widely enough for a skinny girl to get through with no bother. And behind the bars a crawl space, a stone-lined shaft a couple of feet high, disappearing into blackness. It looked as though it had once been a ventilation shaft.

By the side of it, half hidden by the ivy, was a massive iron door that could be slid across to block the shaft entrance, like you'd slide closed a patio door.

I put my hand up to move the ivy, but it began to stir and blow sideways.

I froze. *Get out! Run!* A feeling of danger stronger than I'd ever felt before swept over me, almost making me stumble.

At my side Ant began to cry. "Leon's coming!" he squeaked.

He didn't have to tell me, I could feel it. There was a

change in the air pressure behind me. Before, it had been a gentle breath; now there was a rushing of air. Something was coming down the tunnel toward us, something big enough to carry the air ahead of it in an enormous wave.

I spun around, crouching and ready, and stared into the rushing wind. Something was moving down there, and getting bigger. The ground vibrated.

I had maybe fifteen seconds.

I spat on my hands, fought through the ivy, and pried the old bars apart. One came away easily, as though someone else had discovered this route before me.

"Get in," I shouted. But Ant never moved. He was frozen with fear, looking toward the noise like a rabbit in headlights.

A great gust of hot air splatted me against the dank wall. My shirt flattened itself to my back, my hair blew forward. Ant screamed. With my reptile senses howling, I yanked another iron bar out, picked him up, pushed him through the hole, and threw myself up into the crawl space after him.

Something threw itself at the wall.

"Move!"

Ant scrabbled off down the tunnel. I followed.

Whatever was out there rattling the iron bars was too big to be able to follow. But, sure as hell, I was out of the frying pan and into the fire.

|||

The crawl space in front of me, low to begin with, got even lower before disappearing off into a slimy echoing blackness. But I had to go along it. If it came out in Mrs. Bunn's cellar then I had to seal it off. The last thing I wanted was Java or even a cop infiltrating the place again, and Darcus getting a twitchy finger when it came to his booby traps and blowing the place sky-high.

"Crawl," I ordered, and Ant disappeared off into the blackness like a baby bunny down a rabbit hole. I felt more like a ferret. I was on my hands and knees, crawling through puddles of water on the stone floor. The ceiling was too near the floor, and the sides were too near me. I took deep breaths to steady myself. At first there was a dim light from the corridor behind me, then the tunnel turned a corner and we were into darkness, as though we were crawling through black velvet.

Ant was in front of me. I couldn't see him, but I could sense his movement. It was hard to breathe in here, as if the weight of all the soil above me, the park, the grass, was squashing the air out of the tunnel. My shoulders weren't exactly scraping the sides, but a big man would have struggled.

There was an awkward bend, and for one hellish moment I got my shoulder stuck and thought I was going to end my days stuck underneath the parchmarks on the grass of the park. As I squeezed around I felt a piece of material stuck on the corner of a stone. Someone had come this way before, someone bigger than me, and he'd got stuck and ripped his shirt. Someone in a hurry to escape, maybe. Wren's undercover man who'd disappeared? The man known as Gabriel. A few pieces fit together in my head and I smiled to myself.

I crawled on with quivering knees and my hair wrapped wetly around my face, the walls looming in on me, until I ran into the back of Ant. He'd stopped against a set of iron bars. Light flooded through them. I squeezed by him. On the other side of the bars were boxes of tinned peaches, bags of flour spilling onto the floor, and sacks of potatoes lined against the mildewed walls. Mrs. Bunn's cellar. I was just about to unhook the grille and climb out when I saw a gigantic footprint in the spilled flour.

Wren.

"Snow?" boomed a voice inches away from us. Jeez, he was leaning on the cellar wall right by the crawl space. I put my hand lightly over Ant's mouth, and listened.

"I've checked the cellar . . . nothing. . . . If Java came down here, she's not here now. Just like her brother, she's disappeared off the face of the earth. : . . . I think I'm going to have to call off this whole mission, Freedom's gone AWOL, now we've lost the girl . . . it's taking up too much of our time and we've got other stuff coming in. . . . Whaddya mean, 'Like what?' I've got cases coming out of my ears, these are strange times, my friend, strange times. We've got the Screamer e-mail doing the rounds, kids listen to it and then disappear . . . I've got no leads on that one. . . . And then there's crazy Mrs. Bolt again, still insisting there's a school half a mile below her living room, she can hear the children, she claims. . . . And it's a shame Freedom didn't live up to expectations, I'd have liked to have put him onto Golly Scamp's funfair . . . someone found an old packing case belonging to the fair, and inside there were the skeletons of three pretty weird humans. . . . No, I mean *really* weird, one had a tail, for heaven's sake, and by the size of a leg bone another must have been about eight feet tall. . . . A freak show? No, I think we've got ourselves a DNA reprogramming lab masquerading as a carnival. Ah well, just another day for Phoenix. Yeah, OK, I'll see you soon. I've just got a few ends to tie up and then I'll be in to write a report of the whole fiasco. . . . Ciao."

A shadow crossed in front of the bars. Wren tossed an empty Tic Tac box into the corner and then walked out. I gave it a few minutes, then I nudged Ant to lead the way back out of here. Only he wasn't next to me anymore; he'd slid through the bars into the cellar and was scavenging through the boxes. He arrived back at the bars with a bottle of dandelion and burdock.

"Soda!" he said happily.

We opened the bottle and drank the lot. Dear God, it tasted good, down here in the crawl space. It washed the dust out of our mouths and put some energy back into our limbs. Afterward I reached my hand through the bars and felt around. Just like at the other end, there was a metal door that could be slid across the bars, shutting off the air and the access to the tunnel. That should stop any nosy cop noticing anything.

When we got back to the other end, I checked for Ant's monster, but the coast was clear. We climbed out, and I tugged with all my strength on the rusted iron door. And through my fingers I felt the pulse again. Like everything else in this place, the door was vibrating like a heart. Slowly it squeaked across, covering the crawl space entrance with a thud like the gates of hell clanging shut. I slid a rusted iron pin through a metal loop. Let Wren try to get that open in a hurry.

In another life I could have joined him, helped him chase after his myths and mysteries. But I'd made my choice. Fight, earn some money, and get out. Those were my goals now. And I'd sealed off the last exit to the outside world. Now if Wren searched the cellar and discovered the crawl space, he'd find a dead end. I brushed the rust off my hands and then we made our way back toward the light.

Johnny was at the end of the tunnel with two goons, waiting for me.

"You're a traitor to the fight," he said, dead-eyed.

We stared at each other for a second or two. Java was right. When you looked closely at his eyes, deep down under the confusion, Johnny was still there. And as if to prove it, I felt him slip a piece of paper into my hand.

A glance was all I needed. The handwriting was shaky, but it said: *Please look after Java. I'm in big trouble. Don't listen to what I say. Help me.*

I nodded briefly. And then the two goons strode forward. One knocked me flying. One grabbed Ant, who rewarded his captor with a kick in the leg and a tiny but painful elbow in the stomach. "Don't even twitch," the goon said. "I've got the kid. Give us any grief and –" He shook Ant and then quickly put him down. "Christ, that kid's sticky."

"I'm not moving," I said. "So leave him alone."

"Get up."

I picked myself up slowly. An MP5 was pressed against my neck this time. I sneezed.

"Darcus wants you in the practice arena. And you're in big trouble," said the other goon.

He sounded really happy about the fact.

● ◀ ◀

Wren here, I'm in the cellar of the café.... I want my team down here, fully armed, in five minutes.... I've just located a way into the fight complex, thanks to our boy.... No, he thinks we've called the mission off.... We'll get a team in there, locate him, and then success or failure is up to him....

$$\cancel{||||} \ \cancel{||||} \ \cancel{||||}$$
$$\cancel{||||} \ \cancel{||||} \ \cancel{||||}$$
$$|| \ ||$$

"**P**ractice arena," grunted the goon. He shoved me forward.

I blinked in the bright light. After a short walk we'd reached the hub where all the main tunnels converged on a great circular arena. It stretched out before me, lit by massive overhead floodlights and filled with fighters going through their paces. They were fighting in twos or threes, some with weapons, some with fists, some wearing sparring guards, but most just slugging it out against each other. The air rang with the clash of metal, and with the howls and curses of the men.

It looked like hell, like pandemonium, like we'd gone back to the days of gladiators fighting in the Colosseum. But I couldn't take my eyes away from the sight.

The Tunnel Rats were running here and there, tending to the needs of their fighters like squires did for the knights of old. They were getting water, fetching weapons, flapping towels to cool the fighters down.

Around the outside there was a circular pathway, separated from the fight arena by a low wooden wall. Men in suits were leaning on it, watching the fighters.

These looked like rich and powerful men, some with their sleeves rolled up and their ties loosened, taking notes and shouting among themselves, as though they were checking out horses at a racecourse.

"Quite a sight, isn't it?" said a soft voice in my ear.

It was Rachel. She led me over to the low wall and we looked out over the arena. "It's where the fighters show the punters how good they are, so they'll get plenty of bets, plenty of prize money." She pointed to the center of the arena, where Darcus and a couple of men in dark suits were watching the fighters at close quarters. "He's waiting. I should warn you, he's very hot on discipline. But don't worry, I'll do anything I can to protect you," she said. Then she lowered her voice. "The girl's gone."

I shrugged like I didn't really care, but it was a weight off my mind. There was no way now that Java could get back in.

The goon jabbed me in the back, and as we began walking around the outside path I noticed something that gladdened my heart. Some of the fighters were pulling their punches and faking their throws, like wrestlers do when they look like they're half killing each other and slamming each other around, but there's never any bruises. Seemed like Darcus's brainwashing hadn't worked on everybody, and it cheered me to think that the men and boys could rebel from their life of violence sometimes and decide they didn't want to hurt each other.

"I recognize those features. Smith?"

A punter with a jacket over his shoulder had sauntered by and stopped. He looked at me hard, like you'd look at a rare animal in a zoo.

"Do I know you, mister?" I said.

The man smiled. "Give my regards to your Uncle Shady," he said. "Last time we met, I gave him a three-month sentence." The man chuckled to himself and walked on.

"He's a judge?" I said to Rachel. She nodded. "And he comes here even though this is against the law?"

Rachel looked sadly at me. "Oh, Freedom, you're such an innocent. We are the most exclusive club in the world. The law doesn't come into it. There are politicians, kings, and princes. There are businessmen and film stars. The judge even provides us with fighters. He hands over the men that society can't handle."

I looked closely at the faces going by, and at the men leaning on the wall watching the fighters. I recognized a few of them from the TV and from the front pages of newspapers.

"Ever heard of the Freemasons?" Rachel asked.

I nodded. "Secret club for rich and powerful men. I don't think Gypsies get invited to join, but I've heard of it."

"We are more secret than the Freemasons," she said. "Ever heard how the Mafia kill any member who dares to break their oath of secrecy?" I nodded. Rachel smiled grimly. "We are more brutal than the Mafia."

She looked at the men strolling by us. "A lot of our oldest families *are* Mafia, and they police themselves. If anyone threatens to talk, they silence them," she said quietly. "The rule is, if you talk, you die."

She touched my arm and steered me through a gap in the low wall and out into the arena. I looked at her beautiful face. "How did you get into this, Rachel?"

She gave a bitter smile. "I was born into it. Darcus is my father, I have no choice. I'm trapped." She looked at me sadly. "*You* have a choice, Freedom. Do you feel you've made the right one?"

"I don't know," I said.

◆ ◆ ◆

Out in the middle of the arena, Darcus was watching a couple of fighters flailing at each other with nunchakus. As we approached, he looked up and his yellow eyes began to dance.

"Here he is, Mr. Knight," said the goon, prodding me in the back with his gun. I sneezed again. He rapped me on the head with the gun grip.

"Jeez. Cut it out!" I could have been across the arena before he could even get his finger on the trigger, and down one of the tunnel mouths in about five seconds.

"I wouldn't do anything rash if I were you," said Darcus, reading my mind. "You're late for your first fight, boy."

"I have questions first," I said.

"No, you don't," and this time Darcus's wrecked old voice boomed out. It took me by surprise. I took a step backward, nearly knocking Rachel over. Darcus leaned forward. "You just fight. Here all your questions are answered, all your doubts soothed. Your only concern is the glorious fight." His yellow eyes sparkled. "And the glorious prize money."

And my thoughts of rebelling skittered away like Uncle Shady when the gavvers arrive.

"OK," I said. "I need the money."

"And here is your first opponent," said Darcus, pulling back his lips into a grin. Almost to himself he murmured, "Now let's see what that mutant gene can really do."

I turned around.

Jeez, not him. Anybody but him.

ꟾꟾꟾꟾ ꟾꟾꟾꟾ ꟾꟾꟾꟾ
ꟾꟾꟾꟾ ꟾꟾꟾꟾ ꟾꟾꟾꟾ
ꟾꟾꟾꟾ

Fight? Johnny Sparrow couldn't even stand properly. His eyes were like black pools.

"My blood's on fire," he said. "Fight me."

"He's not fit," I said, staying still.

Darcus gave his vampire smile and opened his hand. On his palm were two pills, one black, one white. "The black is a steroid-based performance enhancer to speed up reflexes, dull the pain center of the brain, and produce massive levels of aggression." He looked up. "The whole thing is my own recipe and very effective. Sometimes too effective."

He held up the white pill. "This is the antidote. We don't want half-crazed fighters roaming around, do we? Care to try them, boy?" His yellow eyes danced. "You will eventually, so why not now?"

I grabbed the pills from his palm and did an overarm throw as far as I could.

"I don't need them!" I said.

"Then fight," said Darcus, and his voice rolled like a heartbeat in my head. Like the heartbeat in the walls. "That is what you're here for. The glorious fight."

But Hercules' face flashed before my eyes, and all the stories I'd heard about him – about how him and me shared something, the same strength, the same outlook – came to me. And it was as though I heard him say, *No, Fredboy, you don't fight like this. Darcus is playing with your mind.*

"You will fight *now*!" shouted Darcus, scattering my thoughts.

I blinked and wiped the sweat from my eyes, and began bouncing on my toes. The fighters with the nunchucks stopped and moved back out of the way. The floor cleared around me and Johnny. More of the fighters stopped, forming a circle around us. Darcus and Rachel, flanked by the goons, were in the front row. The judge and some of the other gamblers had come into the arena, all the better to see me.

To see what, Fredboy? You beat the hell out of another kid who can't even stand upright because of his busted ribs. That ain't proper fighting, that ain't the Smith way.

I shook my head, getting rid of the whisper. I knew what I had to do. I pushed past Johnny and walked over to Darcus.

"I don't want to fight that kid," I said. "I want someone else. A man. Him." I pointed to one of the watchers, a soldier with gold braid hanging off his uniform and a splash of crimson across one torn sleeve. "Him. I'll have him."

Darcus raised his eyebrows. "I think you're getting

ideas above your station," he said. "You don't choose who you fight, I do."

"Why did you choose Johnny Sparrow?" I said. "He's injured."

Darcus's yellow eyes danced. "When you're told to report to me, you come straight here. You do not wander into off-limit tunnels. You've been here less than an hour and already you are proving troublesome," he said, and his voice began rolling again, beating into my brain. "Now get rid of your morals: They're no good here, they won't win you a fortune, so go and fight the glorious fight."

The punters and fighters were silent, drinking in every word and then looking at me curiously. The judge leaned quickly toward his neighbor and spoke behind his hand. Their eyes watched me eagerly.

I turned back to Johnny.

Careful, Fredboy, don't listen to that yellow-eyed gorjer, he's brainwashing you again.

Sometimes it's hard to do the right thing. Sometimes it's easy.

Johnny had got himself into a fancy karate stance, his arms up, ready to attack. Well, one arm was up, anyway. The other one stayed in front of his ribs, protecting the bruise. He came toward me.

"Stop talking and fight me," he said loudly. But in the quietest whisper he said, *"Help."*

"OK!" I growled, and slammed my hand hard across his mouth.

The crowd roared.

And I forced the white pill I'd palmed from Darcus between Johnny's teeth, and tapped him on the jaw to make sure he chewed. His eyes crossed and he staggered.

I stood still, folded my arms, and waited. A couple of the fighters booed me. A nunchuck sliced through the air and whipped across my back. I ignored it all.

"Let the antidote take effect," I muttered when Johnny continued to weave around in front of me.

"Fight!" he said, but deep in his eyes I could see the real Johnny was back, fighting to get control of himself. He pushed me back, and did some fancy footwork and a few quick passes with his hands.

I went flying. The crowd cheered.

I picked myself up off the floor. Java hadn't been joking; Johnny was quick, lightning quick. I could see why he'd got to be All England Champion. I could also see, just from that one throw, how he'd ended up with busted ribs. He was a competition fighter, waiting for the ref to call a foul if anyone cheated, playing by the rules, when there weren't any rules down here.

"I'll throw you," I said to him. "Go down and stay down. Let's end this thing."

The crowd bayed for us to get going. The judge and a few others were scribbling in notebooks. They wanted to see how good I was. They hadn't paid to see two kids dancing around each other, talking.

"Fight me, you coward," Johnny said, in a voice just like Java's. He'd be calling me an oaf next, and saying that we had to bow to each other and shake hands afterward. But then I glanced at him and he gave the smallest of nods.

He danced around, then threw me again. I let him, and the crowd cheered. So I took a turn and brought him down with a flashy shoulder throw. It didn't take much doing. Bird bones, like his sister.

"Java was so worried about you she risked her life to come here," I said under the noise of the crowd. "Now you've got to make the effort to break away." I hung on to him, as though I'd got him in an armlock, but there was no need. He had no strength left.

Around us the crowd had fallen silent. They knew we were faking it and not fighting properly.

A hand fixed on my collar and dragged me backward.

"Mr. Knight wants a word, boy," said a goon.

"Yeah, really?" I said, knocking his hand away from me. "Well, good, because I want a word with him."

Darcus's yellow eyes were still dancing, but it was a dance of death now. I ran over to him and lunged, but a goon grabbed me. Rachel flinched and looked away. The fighters and the punters pushed closer, wanting to hear what was happening.

"Dear boy, you are so untamed," Darcus said, looking mildly amused. "We knew you'd be like a wild animal. It'll take a little longer than usual, and you're going to pull against the harness, but we will break you in the end."

"No way," I said. "You'll never make me fight a kid who can only stand up because you've played with his mind so he doesn't care about the pain."

"Then you'll be punished," said Darcus, smacking his lips with relish. He clicked his fingers, and I saw something move in my peripheral vision.

The hairs stood up on the back of my neck, and I felt myself go into a crouch because, sure as hell, my inner reptile knew what was coming.

Behind me, pushing through the fighters, were the jackals. All five of them. Their eyes blank, honed bodies neat and trim in identical black tracksuits. And as my hackles rose, I knew what it was about them that made my croc senses tingle. Someone had got hold of them and trained them and wiped out everything except their aggression. They had no compassion left. They hadn't got the little voice that whispered to them, telling them to remember to be human, like I had. The little voice that was the real me. The voice that Darcus would take from me, too.

"Did you get them young or were they born here?" I said to him. "Did you brainwash them, too?"

He raised an eyebrow. "We broke them in, like young colts, that's all," he said. "They were tough little thugs when we got them, street urchins, scrapping in the gutters. They would have ended up in prison. But we gave them something to fight for."

And got rid of their souls, I thought.

Darcus's eyes were alight with glee. "There's an easy way, boy: Carry on fighting Johnny – properly. Or there's the hard way: Risk your life against them." He swept a hand toward the jackals. "Your choice, boy. The outcome for us will be the same. You, in the palms of our hands, one way or another."

I looked at Johnny, who was on his feet now. I looked at the excited crowd. The air around me was electric.

Was I a hero or a fighting machine?

Jeez, it would be so much easier to be the baddie. But I couldn't do it, just couldn't fight Johnny. I'd take what was coming to me. Even if it meant all five of the jackals, in their matching black tracksuits. One by one they weren't much of a problem, but all together they were lethal. All with black pools for eyes, unable to keep still.

And worse, I saw a flash of steel in one of the jackals' hands.

"Come on, then," I said to them, and leaped back into the ring.

Five against one, and even then they had to cheat. I thought the flash of steel I'd seen was a knife at first, but it was worse. Handcuffs. A couple of goons grabbed me from behind, and the next minute my hands were cuffed. I was to be chained and baited, and I hadn't even made it to the Bear Pit yet!

"Isn't five against one enough for you, huh?" I shouted.

In the old days the bears had dogs going for their throats. I had the jackals. I kept my chin up, letting them see they couldn't really beat me this way.

"They say you're a freak, that you've been genetically modified," hissed one of them. "We ain't taking any chances."

Then Darcus gave a small signal. And the jackals got to work teaching me a lesson.

It was short and it was nasty. The punters watched it with their eyes narrowed. These were men in love with violence. Like Darcus.

When it stopped they took the handcuffs off. I picked myself up from the floor, and made the best I could of it. Pretended it hadn't hurt. Tucked in my T-shirt, tightened the belt around my jeans, bounced a bit on my feet like it was nothing. Put a smart-aleck smile on my face. Didn't let them see that every part of me was screaming with pain.

One of the jackals'd got himself a gun. He waved it at me, then grabbed my arm.

Darcus licked his lips and steepled his hands. "You see, boy, there's no way out once you come to us."

Rachel looked away. I wondered how she truly felt about her father's business.

I pulled away from the jackal.

"Freedom. My name's Freedom," I said. I pulled the black-and-white photo from my pocket and threw it on the ground at Darcus's feet. "And I want to know how you got this. I don't like being spied on."

I thought he might shout. I thought he might demand to know where I got it from. He did neither. He just gave his death's-head smile.

"Dear boy, we haven't got you here just to fight," he said. "Although, once we've tamed you, the punters will pay thousands to see you. No, we have another reason."

I moved and the jackal waved the gun again, but I knocked his hand back down. "What is it?"

Darcus bared his teeth. "We want the Hercules gene, of course."

"Well, you're not getting it," I said.

ⵌ ⵌ ⵌ ⵌ ⵌ ⵌ ⵌ |

"Let me show you something," said Darcus, struggling to keep his temper.

He gave a signal to Rachel and we threaded our way across the arena and into the mouth of one of the tunnels. Or what I thought was one of the tunnels.

Darcus stopped me on the threshold. "This is our temple," he said, his voice no longer rolling and powerful. It was hushed. "Our holy of holies. Don't try anything in here."

It was like a black cave, but I think it must have been an old furnace from the chemical works. Maybe it was where they used to cook up the acids, because the air stung my eyes and tasted like tin. The domed ceiling and brick walls were black and covered with photos, old sepia-tinted ones at the far end and computer printouts nearest to us. On one side there were photos of the fighters – the last one was of Johnny's face, bleached by the flash of the camera. On the other wall there were pictures of men, some that you'd know from TV and the movies. Every so often a face had been scratched out.

Along the walls there were glass cabinets, the sort

you'd find in a museum. And at the far end a flame flickered from a black holder, like the Olympic torch. Darcus went up to it and knelt by it.

"This is our eternal flame," he breathed. "As long as the fight continues, it will remain alight."

Now I understood Darcus. He wasn't just the organizer of the fight, he was the priest. This was his religion. I risked a glance at Rachel. She was watching the flame, too, and her eyes sparkled. I thought at the time it was tears.

"This is where we swear allegiance to the fight," said Darcus. "Our guests leave us a token as proof of their sincerity." He waved his ice-cold hand at the photos.

"And the people with their faces scratched out?" I asked.

Darcus pointed to an old faded portrait of a man with a beard like a haystack. His face and the ones of the men next to him were scratched out. "In 1872 Captain Briggs leaked details of the fight to his crew. The next week Briggs and his men disappeared off the face of the earth. You've probably heard of him."

"No," I said bleakly.

"Really?" Darcus gave a death grin. "His ship was the *Marie Celeste*. Even in the middle of the Atlantic Ocean, Briggs wasn't safe from our retribution."

I narrowed my eyes. "You're telling me this fight's been running for hundreds of years?"

Darcus examined a fingernail, and then looked up at

me. "Years? We don't measure in years, boy, we measure in *eras*. And to amuse our gamblers, each era has a different historical theme." He waved a hand to take in the photos of all the fighters. "This is the era of the Bear Pit, that's all you need to know."

"So how many other eras have there been?"

"More than you'd ever imagine in your wildest dreams," said Darcus. "I'm very old, and even I don't know how many." I glanced at him. His head was almost mummified when you looked closely. My skin crawled.

I looked along the rows of photos. "So each person with their face scratched out was murdered by your goons?"

"Not murder. Retribution for a broken oath."

I stopped before a photo of a Chinese man, small but muscled like a terrier. A hero of mine, a fighter like no other. His face was missing. "Bruce Lee, the best in the world, fell to you?" I said, like I couldn't believe it. But in my heart I did.

Darcus tore the photo down and ripped it in half. "He came here once and disapproved. He, of all people, should have understood our glorious fight." His voice broke. "But he caused us endless trouble. It was not to be tolerated."

He walked over to a glass cabinet lit by spotlights and full of bleached white bones and skulls. He caressed the glass with his hand. "These are the relics of our best fighters. The champions of champions." He ran his hand along the line of photos above the cabinet. "Even after death they are treated as heroes." His hand continued until it came to a photo above another cabinet.

It was a very old photo, faded and creased, of a man with a handlebar mustache and a lionskin draped over one shoulder.

"And then there was Hercules Smith," said Darcus, and showed his teeth like a wolf.

Dear God, Hercules had fought for these people? Last time I'd seen a copy of this same photo I was sitting with Whitney Jade, not knowing my life was about to change. I looked at my ancestor as he stared into the camera, the lion's head against his massive chest, and my heart sank. I wanted to rip the photo from the wall and get it away from this place. I stopped myself. I wouldn't give Darcus the pleasure of seeing me react.

Then I noticed what was in the cabinet. "Jeez, is this a relic as well?" I asked.

It was a pigtail of human hair, black as night.

"It's Hercules' hair," said Darcus. "The men saved it because they worshiped him. They didn't know that a couple of centuries later we would use it to create another fighter, with the same rogue gene." He glanced at me. "Do you even know what a gene is, boy?"

"If you inherit blue-eyed genes you get blue eyes," I said, thanks to Java.

"That's right," he said. "But sometimes people are born with rogue genes, one-offs, little mistakes in the

DNA that make them extraordinary. If it's a gene that controls strength, then you get Hercules."

I said nothing.

"And you have it, boy. We watched you. Then we lost you. And now you turn up on our doorstep, bringing us trouble. Just like your ancestor." He pointed to the photo of Hercules again. "He was trouble from the word go, too. No discipline."

"He was a traveling man," I said. "We don't take orders."

Darcus ignored me. "His was the era of the Roman gladiators. They'd styled the fight arena to look like a Roman amphitheater, and the fighters wore leather armor and fought with short swords. It was a fitting era for a man named after a Roman god."

His eyes grew bloodthirsty. Rachel looked away, fiddling with her bracelet. "There were lions and wild creatures in those days. And men were pitted against them. Hercules fought a lion once. He was like a god. The men stood in awe of him."

And in my mind I heard old Hercules say, *Who, me, fight for that yellow-eyed gorjer all my life? No chance!*

"But he didn't fight for you for long, did he?" I said craftily. And Darcus stopped smiling.

Rachel stepped forward. "One day a jealous fighter cut off his long hair as he slept, hoping it would weaken him. Hercules was the champion of champions, so of course the fighter was put to death. When Hercules heard, he went on the rampage and fought his way out. Even while he wrecked the fight the men looked on him with admiration."

I looked at the photo and nodded slowly. I should have known Hercules had been the good guy in the end. Like me, he'd joined the fight. But only until he realized he'd made a mistake.

Darcus shrugged. "We lost him, but we watched his sons and their sons. We wanted another Hercules, but we wanted to catch him early so that we could teach him the ways of the fight."

He opened the case, took out the hank of black hair, and stroked it like a cat.

"But a rogue gene is just that," he continued. "Rogue. Unpredictable. But then came the time of genetic engineering." He pulled out one of the hairs from the pigtail and held it up in the flame's light. "Twenty years ago we found we could take the rogue gene from the DNA in just one hair and splice it into another human being. And make another god with Hercules' strength."

I laughed in disbelief. The man was crazy. "No. That wasn't possible twenty years ago. It's not even possible now."

Darcus smiled like I was a fool. "You listen to the news too much. Law-abiding scientists say it isn't. Criminals, governments, and the military secretly know differently."

"So show me this clone of Hercules," I said.

Darcus leaned his hand against another photo. It showed a tall, well-muscled fighter with long dark hair and burning eyes. He looked like a rock star with his tight pants and bare chest. "This is Leon. Our best fighter. A phenomenon." His eyes lingered on the photo for a moment. "Amazing strength and bravery. We bred him ourselves."

"I want to meet him," I said, wrapping my arms around myself for warmth. The icy wind blowing through the temple was chilling me to the bone.

Rachel put a hand on my arm. "You can't," she said. "For a while it worked, but then he began to get weaker and he became unpredictable." She glanced at Darcus. "So ten years ago we tried splicing with a new source of the rogue gene –"

Dear God! I didn't give her time to finish. "Ten years ago?" I said, and my mind wound backward. To a man grabbing me, and then a pain in my arm. Blood on my sleeve and a triangular scar. *We only lost you once*, Snow had said.

"Damn you to hell, Darcus, you used my blood to fix Leon!"

Darcus inclined his head as though I'd complimented him. "I suppose you could almost say he's your brother!" And his eyes danced over my face. He wanted to see me react, but he was disappointed. My face was like stone now. He sighed. "But it was all to no avail, I'm afraid.

Leon, unfortunately, has not been a success. In fact he's become rather an embarrassment to us."

But I wasn't listening anymore. "The monster in the tunnel, the one who scares the little kids. It's Leon? You made a monster?"

Darcus gave a shrug, like it was no big deal. He could've been discussing how he'd made buttered toast and it'd gone a bit wrong. "We can splice and for a while it works. But there are always complications." He looked at me and his eyes danced again. "That's why we need that rogue gene of yours again. We need to start from scratch." He smiled. "Of course, we're going to need to experiment quite a bit, so stealing some of your blood is not an option this time. We need it on tap, fresh from a living body. And we need to watch you fight, evaluate your strengths, work out how to eliminate your bad points, the wildness." He tapped my cheek. "At the moment you won't like the idea. But by the time we've finished, you'll no longer be Freedom Smith, you'll be our creature to do with as we wish."

I shrugged away from him, making sure I moved closer to Rachel. "Brainwashing? Is that what you're going to do to me? Is that how you get the fighters to go on with the glorious fight, even when their ribs are busted?" I said, my fists clenching. "It's not just performance enhancers, is it, Darcus? Or am I the only one to have spotted the elf?"

Rachel gave a small laugh. "An elf? Really, Freedom, I don't think we have any elves."

"Put your hand on any of the walls and feel the heartbeat," I said, my eyes not leaving Darcus's. "That's an elf. An extra-low-frequency sound. It puts your brain into an alpha trance state, and then a shrewd man with a rolling voice, speaking in time to your heartbeat, can tell you anything and you'll believe it like it's the truth."

Darcus bared his teeth again.

"How shrewd of you! You really are a force to be reckoned with," he said admiringly. "Things tend to drag a little over the eras, but now I think you're going to provide us with a few fireworks before we break you."

"Sorry to disappoint you," I said, and grabbed Rachel. She swore softly.

"Keep back," I warned. I didn't like taking a hostage. But it was the only way I was going to get out of the place without someone shooting me. "I'll never fight for you. And you'll never experiment on me."

But Darcus only bared his teeth some more.

"Did you really think it would be that easy?" he said. He picked up a remote, and a plasma screen in the corner blinked on. I felt Rachel gasp. "I think you should watch this."

It was a view from a CCTV camera.

Something was moving along an old tunnel. The thing was huge and hunched over. After a few steps it stopped to sniff the air. Then it began to move more quickly and with purpose. The hair on the nape of my neck stood on end. This was the body language of a hunter.

Darcus clicked the remote and the picture changed. This one showed a curved wall, flooded with light from a moving spotlight somewhere beyond the camera. And in the center, Java and Ant, eyes glowing.

Darcus steepled his hands and looked over them, straight at me.

"Look!" he said with his death grin. "Your brother Leon's got a couple of new playmates waiting for him in the Bear Pit." He put his head to one side. "*Now* will you fight?"

```
卌 卌 卌
卌 卌 卌
卌 ||
```

| ran. I left the "temple" behind. I came to the wooden wall surrounding the arena. I could've jumped it but I kicked at it. And kept kicking. When a panel splintered and then fell to the floor, I stamped on it until a piece of wood the size of a baseball bat snapped off. Now I had a weapon.

I leaped the smashed barrier and ran across the arena and into a tunnel on the other side. Punters scattered before me. Fighters watched me go by with their eyes narrowed, then began to follow.

The Bear Pit was on the floor above. I had to get to the elevator fast. I let the twists and turns I'd memorized earlier flood back, and my feet began to find their own way.

I ran through the darkness. There was a howling in my ears and I didn't know whether it was the blood rushing to my brain or the hot wind slicing through the tunnel. Water lay in deep puddles on the tunnel floor, treacherous with slime and mold. I slashed out with the wooden club at the vines and creepers that hung in my way. Jeez, I was consumed by fear and anger. My blood was on fire, my skin burned, but it wasn't because of Darcus's steroids.

I swear I'd never run this fast before. I counted my steps, turned, and flew down a tunnel, one of the main spokes that led straight back to the elevator. Every second seemed like a lifetime, but then there was a light ahead of me and I was storming out into the circular outer tunnel. I raced for the elevator doors.

Inside, I punched the button for the next floor. The elevator jerked upward. After what seemed like an eternity the BEAR PIT sign lit up and the bell pinged. The doors opened and I thanked my lucky stars – the layout up here was identical to the practice level, which meant the central arena would be the Bear Pit.

I began to run. No, it was more than a run; I flew. Far ahead of me I heard the howl again. I sniffed the air, just as the crouched shadow had. I caught the scent again, the scent of a monster, wafting down the tunnels toward me. I let my reptile senses take over.

A light at the end of the tunnel. I couldn't be far away. There were punters hurrying ahead of me, making their way to the Bear Pit. Then an arm like a steel bar appeared in front of me. I ran into it and jerked to a halt. But only for a second.

"This way is for punters only," said a goon. "Fighters go down there."

And I was off and racing down a bleak tunnel covered in the graffitied boasts and curses of all the men and boys who'd come this way to fight.

"This is a special announcement," said Darcus's rolling voice from speakers on the tunnel walls. "We have been infiltrated, but there is nothing to worry about, gentlemen. The fight will be safe, you will be safe. The female intruder has been apprehended. Her fate is to face Leon. And for your entertainment the Gypsy boy, Freedom Smith, will be fighting to save her life. Either he will kill Leon or she will pay for her transgression. Gentlemen, blood will be spilled tonight. Please make your way to the pit!"

I ran on down the tunnel, Darcus's hellfire preacher voice echoing around me. There was the noise of men shouting up ahead. An iron gate grated upward. Ice ran along my spine now, my hackles rose, and the adrenaline started to pump. The reptile in me was getting ready to survive.

I walked into the arena feeling small and insignificant, like a lone gladiator entering the Colosseum. The iron gate slammed down behind me.

"Welcome, Freedom Smith," said the loudspeaker. "Welcome to the Bear Pit."

A roar went up from the crowd above.

Jeez, it was like the practice arena on the floor below – the same massive circular space, the same blinding lights – but it was a hundred times worse. In the center of the arena was the Bear Pit, and I was trapped inside it.

The pit was about fifteen feet deep and twenty paces across, with smooth sides and a curved floor, like a gigantic basin. The sort of thing that skateboarders do their tricks in. Except that this one had a wooden stake in the middle, where in the old days a bear would've been chained. The top was ringed with gamblers leaning over and bellowing for my blood. It was worse than any boxing ring. Worse than ropes. Worse than the crawl space. I walked into the middle, my scalp creeping and my skin cold.

Above me, a spider's web of gantries and walkways crisscrossed the high vaulted ceiling. Punters were strolling along them or leaning over the railings to get a bird's-eye view of the mayhem below. I thought for a moment that there were bears on the walkways, too, but when I looked again they turned out to be women in huge fur coats, diamonds shining around their necks and on their hands as they clapped and shouted, as avidly as the men.

Banks of seats circled the pit, tier after tier rising higher, filled with men, arguing and shouting, reaching over each other, money changing hands. Cigarette smoke writhed up toward a blackened ceiling.

Floodlights illuminated the pit, throwing the edges of the watching crowd into darkness. The whole thing, the Bear Pit, the shouting, the gamblers on the gantries and walkways craning their necks to see, the smell of sweat and blood – it was electric, mesmerizing, terrible.

I looked up, sweating, into a circle of faces. Darcus was leaning on the wall surrounding the pit with a bodyguard of jackals, smiling down at me. But I hardly gave them a second glance, because chained by a hand to the wooden stake in the center of the pit stood Java, feet planted, eyes blazing. Ant was holding her hand. And I could hear the iron gate being raised again.

The ground began to tremble, and above the noise of the crowd came an almighty roar.

"Behind you!" shouted Java.

I turned around.

"Dear Lord, we're dead," I breathed.

‖‖ ‖‖ ‖‖
‖‖ ‖‖ ‖‖
‖‖ |||

Leon ducked under the iron gate and it clanged shut. He still had the long dark hair I'd seen in the photo, except now it was in dreadlocks hanging down his back. But everything else about him had changed.

He was bigger than a sumo, and dressed in greasy stained leather like a Roman gladiator. His head had grown enormous, with great bulges in the skull. His eyes had disappeared into the flesh, until just two small puckers showed. He'd once been muscled like an athlete, but now he was all twisted and his body had grown huge in different places, and shrunk in others. And there was something very wrong with his skin. It was gray and thick and lying in folds like the hide of a great beast. It had patches of furry green and brown, as though the fungus on the walls had grown on his flesh.

I looked at the wooden club I held. It would be like trying to knock out an elephant with a matchstick.

In the depths of his scarred and puffed face two shiny beads, like spiders' eyes, blinked at me. The thundering of his breath filled the pit.

"We're not dead yet," Java shouted desperately to me. She was trying to wriggle her hand out of the shackle. "They're saying that Leon's your brother. I don't know how that can be. But if that's true, Freedom, it's got to mean something."

"Fee, fi, fo, fum," said Leon, circling us, his hair flying.

"Jeez, have you seen the state of him?" I said, whirling around, trying to keep him in sight.

"Talk to him!" said Java. "It's the only hope we have!"

Behind me Ant said, "Get the naughty monster, Freedom," like he still thought I was his knight in shining armor.

And Leon heard, and growled, "I eat little boys!" and then gave a laugh like a lion roaring.

But all I could think about was the fear in my gut. And that Leon had become like this because of the Hercules gene. My gene. Java was wrong. I couldn't tell him.

"Leon?" I shouted. "What do you want with me?"

His face was a slab of flesh with no mouth visible. But from somewhere came a voice.

"I just want to talk," he rumbled. "I'm so lonely. Am I too hideous for you to talk to me?"

I swallowed. "No, Leon, we can talk."

He made a noise. It took me a few seconds to realize he was chuckling.

"Only joking," he growled. "The kid'll do for starters,

but the girl looks interesting, too. I'll grind their bones to make my bread!"

"Why do this?" I said, circling, keeping between him and Java, giving myself time to find a way to attack him.

"To stop the pain," came Leon's voice from the folds of gray skin. High above me, on the edge of the pit, a jackal laughed.

"Yeah, right, attacking us will stop the pain!" I shouted, walking backward and forward, trying to find a weakness, anything.

The mountain of flesh trembled. "It doesn't stop the pain, but I enjoy it."

He made a lunge for Ant. The little boy darted away, but the chain around his wrist jerked him back and Java grabbed him and pulled him around the wooden post.

I gripped my club. "Leave them alone!" I shouted. I swung it high and it smacked against his huge shoulders. I swung again and again. "It's me you're fighting!" He staggered backward, laughing at me, hardly feeling the blows. But I saw my chance.

"Scared of me, are you?" I shouted, still beating him back. And he laughed, swatting away my club as though it was an irritating fly. Two more steps and he'd backed into the iron gate.

"Oh, I'm so scared!" he mocked, leaning back against the bars. This was my chance. I leaped forward and grabbed a dreadlock, wrapped it around one of the iron bars, and knotted it.

"Laugh all you want now!" I said, leaping away.

Leon tried to follow me, then his head whipped back, fixed by his hair to the bar. He howled in rage and anguish.

I took a run across the floor of the pit and did three or four vertical steps up its sheer stone side and grabbed for the edge. I pulled myself up. Darcus smiled, but the jackals moved closer to him.

"Let's talk," I said. "Let the girl and the little kid go, and you can do what you want with me."

His face loomed close to me. "Dear boy! But why should I? Leon won't leave the Bear Pit without his fight. Our fun will be seeing you try to defend the girl in the face of Leon's monstrous strength. If I let her and the little boy go, then he'll kill you instead."

Darcus put his cold claw on my head. I couldn't brush him off. "We don't want you dead, boy, we have too many exciting experiments to try on you. You'll never get out of here. By tomorrow you won't even want to."

The jackal next to him laughed.

Was this my fate? Darcus stealing my soul, turning me into a jackal, too?

Suddenly Darcus grabbed my hair and then pushed. "Fight!" he roared, and I fell back into the pit.

So this was the edge.

The air around us was electric. Gamblers were fighting each other to see this battle. Voices were shouting, screaming at us to fight, fists waving, adrenaline soaking into the air. The walls of the pit rose up all around me, but there was no time to worry about the pain in my guts and the eyes staring down at me.

With a mighty howl, Leon ripped the dreadlock from his head and left it hanging on the bars. He circled Java and Ant again. Java had Ant by the hand and they were trying to keep the post between themselves and Leon, but their chains weren't long enough.

Leon and I began a monstrous dance. Me circling, crouched and wary, trying to see if there was a weak point on him, Leon shuffling around to keep me in view, slobbering and mumbling to himself, his great bulk trembling.

"Tell him, you idiot!" Java screamed. "Tell him you're brothers!"

I had nothing to lose. "Did you hear that, Leon? Me and you, we're brothers," I shouted.

That stopped him for a moment. "Brothers?" jeered Leon. "We're not brothers, I'm a one-off. There's only one Leon." He thumped his massive chest like a gorilla. "Rachel told me that they made me."

He swung a punch at me again. I feinted left and went right, then hit out again with the club, but his hide was like a bulletproof Kevlar vest, completely impenetrable. He wouldn't feel even the hardest blow. He was unbeatable.

"You're wrong, Leon," I said beneath the noise of the crowd. "They made you using our granddaddy's genes.

And then they added my blood. You're not a monster. You're a kinsman, Leon, you're a Smith!"

Leon took a step forward that shook the ground, and then one back. I'd confused him at least. "What's a Smith?" he growled.

"You are! And so am I. We share a great-great-great-granddaddy, Leon. Old Hercules. That's why we're strong. And we're Gypsies, Leon, we don't lose our kith and kin, we stay with them."

He started pacing, like a caged tiger does, and shaking his head as if his brain was hurting. "Hercules? I know Hercules." He stopped and thumped me in the chest. "How do *you* know Hercules?"

"He's family," I shouted. "Mine, and yours!"

"Fee, fi, fo, fum, I'm a monster, not a brother. . . ." he muttered as he started pacing again.

I kept very still, hoping he'd work it out for himself. But just when I thought he'd calmed down, he turned and roared, "You're trying to trick me!"

He stamped his huge foot. The ground shook. And an idea struck me like lightning. It might not work, but I had nothing to lose.

"Leon, I can prove I'm not lying," I shouted. "I know something about you, something only another Smith would know!"

Leon stopped in front of me and lowered his head, snorting like a bull about to charge. "No more lies!" he shouted, striding toward me menacingly.

"Listen to me!" I pleaded, backing away. "Listen. I'm willing to bet on my life that you've got webbed toes on your left foot!" My back hit the wall of the Bear Pit. Leon loomed over me. "Webbed toes are a sign of a Smith. I've got them! Our ancestors had them." Desperately, I kicked off my sneaker. *"Look!"*

Leon took a step back, staring at my foot. For a second I thought I'd guessed right, that he did have the Smith toes. But I was wrong. He grabbed my arm and threw me to the other side of the pit. I landed winded. Flat on my back and helpless as a baby.

I heard Java cry out, "No, get up! He's coming for you!" I saw Darcus signal to the goons to stop Leon, but they were too late. I had no breath, I couldn't move. Leon had only to stamp his foot down or snap me like a twig and I'd be a goner.

The crowd went wild. Leon leaped for the side of the pit above me and held on with one hand. He hung there, above my head, and roared in anger.

"Old Hercules would've taken care of you, Leon," I croaked desperately, looking up at him. "He'd have punched his way out of here and taken you away. Smiths always look after Smiths."

But it was too late.

Leon let go, and his four-hundred-plus pounds slammed down on top of me.

was dead. There was only blackness. Leon's bulk had blotted out the light and crushed me. I was dead, but for some reason I was still breathing.

"Ha!" said Leon quietly, from above. "Leon's five-star monster splash!"

God help him, he'd done a body splash! He'd pulled a wrestling move on me. His leap should've killed me, but wrestlers learn to fake it. They slam with their arms and legs, and the noise is bad, but their weight never touches the victim underneath.

Leon had landed on me and I'd felt nothing. But my heart was pounding nineteen to the dozen, and I couldn't have stood up if I'd tried.

"Bet that scared you," he whispered. "You didn't know I could wrestle, did you?" He shifted his bulk and knelt up, but his breathing was bad now. Even one small body splash had taken its toll. I think it was his heart. Smiths are born to be lithe and strong, not the size of mammoths. Leon had been carrying his monstrous weight around for too long.

"Darcus makes me fight the men," he panted. "I don't want to kill 'em. So they taught me wrestling."

I got slowly to my feet, pretending he'd knocked the wind from me and smashed my ribs.

"The men laugh at my toes, but you got 'em, too!" he panted. "I'm not a one-off. I've got family."

I grinned at him, but I kept my distance, like you would from a dangerous dog that's just started to wag its tail but is still showing its teeth. "You're a Smith."

A coin hit me on the back of the neck, and then another. The crowd wanted action. Before I could move, Leon reached out and did a suplex on me, followed by an airplane spin and a cannonball splash. The crowd went wild, but Darcus wasn't cheering.

"Fight properly or there'll be trouble, Leon!" he shouted.

Leon looked up, flinched, and then reached over with his massive hand and grabbed the chains holding Java and Ant.

Dear God, he was going to kill them.

"No, Leon!" I shouted.

But he grabbed their chains and pulled, and there was a creak, and the bolts holding the chains popped and Java and Ant were free. They ran to the side of the pit, Java shielding Ant.

"Good man," I hissed. "See, I told you, you're a Smith:

You ain't only got old Hercules' genes, you've got his fair play and his spirit!"

Leon's tiny eyes sought mine.

"My brain's not right. Sometimes I see a red mist over everything and I want to fight and hurt things. I'm not safe." He blinked. "In a part of my mind, you're a brother, and I'm a Smith, but in the other, everything's red and all I want to do is fight. . . ."

"Leon, when we get out of here, I'll make sure the red goes away. Darcus has made you go mad. We'll get you away from him."

He dragged me up by the scruff of my neck and then did a flying leg roll-up, and although it nearly snapped my spine I knew he was trying not to hurt me. He was breathing very badly now, though. He stumbled, and I had to hold him up and pretend it was him holding me up.

"Let's give 'em a Smith fight, huh, Leon, me and you, show how it's done, make old Hercules proud of us, yes? The Smith brothers, the ultimate wrestling team," I said. And although he shook his head and bellowed, maybe I glimpsed a light in his eyes that wasn't there a minute ago.

And so we were the Smith brothers for a minute or two. And the ring echoed with thuds and growls and screams, and the crowd was fooled and yelled for more.

But Darcus knew. All of a sudden, above the roaring of the crowd, I heard Darcus's voice, and I glanced up.

He had a mike to his mouth, and his voice was rolling out across the Bear Pit.

"Bad boy, Leon. You know what happens to bad fighters, Leon? More pain!" And one of the jackals whipped out a police-issue Taser stun gun and fired it down into the pit. The dart hit Leon in the shoulder, and a bolt of electricity flew down the wire and threw him backward. It should have knocked him down or temporarily paralyzed him. But this was Leon. He dragged the dart out of his shoulder and threw it away. Then he got to his feet with a terrible slowness and looked around till he saw me. The whites of his eyes had gone red, and his breathing sounded like wild growling. Lord knows how many times they'd taunted him with the Taser, making him go crazy like a circus animal that learns to do tricks with whips and kicks. "Leon, remember, I'll take you away from this, from Darcus and the pain," I said, watching him as if he were a dangerous animal.

But it was too late. The Taser had done its work. Leon was only seeing red.

"Fee, fi, fo!" he yelled, and then he launched himself at me.

Next thing I knew I was flying, and I landed, legs tangled, in a crumpled heap, kicking myself on the ankle and smashing my head against the pit wall. The world blurred.

Jesus, Fredboy, don't lose consciousness now! He's seeing red, you've got to fight him!

I picked myself up, shaking my head, trying to focus my eyes, the crowd baying at me, and I launched myself at Leon again. My wooden club beat a tattoo on his skull, but it made no difference. I bounced off the walls, I somersaulted off his colossal bulk. Java ducked and dived around the pit, dragging her chains, hanging on to Ant. But nothing I did could touch him. I gathered my strength and swung the club, but Leon just swatted me away. I flew and skidded across the pit, the wall knocking the wind out of me. I tried to stand. I got as far as my knees. I couldn't get farther. I crouched down and gasped for breath.

There was no way to stop him; he was invincible. He was going to get his kill, Java and Ant would die, and there was nothing I could do.

Old Hercules would have walked away in disgust. I had the Hercules gene and it was going to make no difference.

Bury me standing, the old traveler men used to say when things went wrong. *Bury me standing, I've been on my knees all my life.*

And I always laughed when I heard this, because I thought there was no way anyone would get me on my knees. But I was wrong, because here I was at the bottom of the pit, bloodied and scared. And the Leon who wasn't my brother knew it.

While I gasped for breath, he moved like lightning across the pit. It should have been impossible for him to run like that, but I was forgetting the rogue gene. Just because it had gone wrong didn't mean he hadn't still got the power and the strength. No wonder they left him to roam the tunnels unchecked.

In two gigantic strides he'd grabbed Ant and Java and was swinging them from his hands as though they weighed nothing.

"Mine!" he crowed. And I froze, because he could break them like twigs and I was powerless to stop it.

Jeez, Fredboy, old Hercules would have thought of something. He never quit – ninety rounds and the blood running down him and he'd still be fighting and plotting!

I picked myself up, my arms wide to show I meant no harm, and crouched a little, making myself smaller and less of a threat. Let him see that he needn't hurt them. Ant was like a baby rabbit caught by the scruff of the neck, his eyes on me, his knight in shining armor. Some knight I was turning out to be.

"It's not them you should be attacking, it's me," I said, dropping the club. "They used my blood, my DNA, to give you strength. I'm the reason you're like this." I beckoned him with my hand. "Put them down. Fight me first."

For a second nothing happened, then he threw Ant and Java down behind him. He put his head back and screamed in fury at me.

And my reptile senses saw something. Only I didn't know what it was yet.

"You're a monster!" I shouted. "Fight!"

Leon roared. There it was again! The skin under his chin wasn't thickened – it was normal skin, white like an uncooked chicken, not hide.

He paced around me, shaking his head, saliva flying everywhere. The noise level dropped to zero. The gamblers around the edge, the men on the gantries leaned over to see, all eyes on us.

Don't think about the eyes, I told myself. *Just concentrate on surviving.*

Leon was circling like a wild animal would, tiny eyes glinting crimson in the light. Circling. Biding his time.

Time to jive.

"You know the problem with Gypsies?" I said, breathing deep, pulling air into my lungs. Leon stared at me.

"What?" he rumbled.

"We're never where people think we should be, and always where they don't want us. We always do something different. And that gets people really mad."

He came flying at me, gathering speed as he crossed the pit, like a runaway horse.

On he came, and then I wasn't there anymore. I did what I'd do to any runaway horse. Dodge to one side at the last minute, then grab its mane and fling myself onto its back. Stow Fair had taught me many things that Darcus hadn't captured on his camera.

Leon bellowed in rage and tried to reach around. I clung to his back, grabbed his long dreadlocks, threw them around his neck where the skin was soft, and pulled.

For a full minute nothing much happened. We stayed perfectly balanced. Me on his back, feet braced against him, leaning back with all my weight, while he pulled forward, choking himself on his own hair. Without breath he would have to slow down and calm down. Then maybe he'd recognize me again.

For a whole minute we stayed like that. Then he overbalanced just a little and we began tottering around in an eerie dance, Leon's hands grabbing at the air and his eyes wide. Angry grunts came from his throat. I felt his knees buckle.

He should have gone down. Instead he went up.

With a massive surge of power Leon jackknifed and grabbed for the top of the pit, caught it, and pulled himself up. The punters scattered as his monstrous head rose above the wall, with me clinging like a monkey to his back. And then he threw himself backward.

A split second and I was going to be squashed like a bug by Leon's bulk. But there was something he didn't realize: I'd had enough of tight spaces. Don't bury me standing, don't bury me at all. I thought of old Hercules, fighting ninety rounds with his legs buckling under him but always managing to pull out that one last punch.

As Leon slammed back toward the floor I threw myself backward, just as he landed with a thud that stopped the noise around the arena dead.

It was a thud that stopped Leon, too. He lay on the floor of the pit, out cold, his breath wheezing.

"Sorry, Leon," I said. But there was nothing more I could do. I looked up. Darcus was gone.

"Satisfied?" I shouted to the punters. No one moved. The whole place was deathly quiet. "You've had your bloodlust fix for today," I said. "Now, who's going to help us out?"

A hand reached down. "For Christ's sake, Java, Dad'll kill us both!" said Johnny Sparrow, pulling his sister out of the pit. Which I suppose meant he was back to normal. At least his eyes were blue again, like his sister's.

A few more hands came over the top. It was the Rats. And behind them, some of the older boys, similar in age to me. "Something's happening!" said one of them, his eyes sparkling.

I looked at all the boys, with their bruises and their tattered clothes, and I thought, *Jeez, even when someone gets brought up in the worst sort of fight in the world, and given pills and brainwashed, there's still something inside that's good.*

But I had no idea what to do next. The Rats were staring at me. So were the gamblers. Then a voice rang out.

"Freedom!"

A figure, outlined by the spotlights, swung down from one of the gantries, a cigar clamped between his teeth and something trailing smoke in his hand.

No. This only happened in the movies.

"Is it tomorrow?" said Ant hopefully.

Then everything went black, and the screaming began.

Thick smoke rolled over the arena. A flash of light came from above, and I saw Wren running toward us with another grenade. As he threw it, there was a soft thud and more smoke, and screams and howls of rage started up on the other side of the pit.

Wren put out a huge arm and scooped us all up against a wall, away from the panicking punters. We crouched down out of the way, the Rats and Ant hiding behind us, the older boys huddled next to us.

"How?" I asked.

He held out a device, sleek and deceptively simple. "Congratulations, you've just proved that the Nanny chip works." He moved the cigar to the other side of his mouth and tapped the device. It beeped at him.

"Global Positioning System linked to the mobile phone network. Pinpoints your position to the last inch. We've been following your every move since the fight in Mrs. Bunn's." He grinned through the smoke. "After I gave you the painkiller with a Nanny chip implanted in it. Your trek down the crawl space gave us the perfect way into the fight." He hoisted what looked like a rocket launcher onto his shoulder. "But thanks to your handiwork with the iron door, I needed a little help from this baby!" He patted its gleaming side. "M1500 hand cannon. Military issue."

He dragged me out of the path of a group of cops with riot shields as they forced their way through the smoke-shrouded crowds. He grabbed the last one.

"Jonesy, this place is like a rabbit warren, make sure you check all the tunnels and watch out for anyone escaping through secret exits."

"We'll show him!" said one of the older boys. "We know our way around here, even in the dark!"

"Follow us!" shouted another. They disappeared into the fog, part of the police operation now. Talk about a change of fortunes.

Wren looked me in the eye. Boy, was he good at that. I felt like he was looking straight into my soul. "But all this will come to nothing if no one talks. They'll claim it's a film set and Darcus will go free to start again somewhere else, unless someone has the courage to break the silence around the fight and stand up and condemn him."

He looked at me. "Have you got the guts to testify against Darcus?"

I thought of Leon, my brother, a mutant through no fault of his own, and the photos with the faces scratched out, the bones of the fighters who'd never known anything but the fight. I didn't even have to think it over. "Just watch me," I said quietly.

And I could tell by the two small lines going upward on either side of his mouth that Wren was pleased with me, and I'd done good and redeemed myself. But there was no time to be pleased with myself. Things were heating up around us.

"Can we get out of this hellhole now?" I said. I needed fresh air like Uncle Shady needed a pint.

The smoke was getting thicker, and visibility was down to a couple of feet. I was going to die of claustrophobia if we didn't move.

"Put these on," said Wren, handing out green goggles. When I looked again I could see straight across the Bear Pit. Fighting had broken out over the gantries and walkways. Police in flak jackets were pouring in from all sides, wading through the battles, stirring up the dust and smoke.

Fighters and gamblers streamed by us, trying to get out of the pit and into the tunnels. "Set up an evacuation action and drive 'em upstairs," Wren yelled into a walkie-talkie. "When we followed your tracer on our monitor and found the secret way in, we set up an infiltration operation. We've got half the county's police force waiting outside!"

Wren pushed the cannon into my hands and thrust me forward; then he grabbed Johnny, who was leaning over and holding his ribs. "Java, keep the kids with you; hold hands so they don't get lost. We've got to get out of here fast." He started shouting into his earpiece, then turned and bellowed at me. "Damn! They can't find Darcus! He's disappeared. We've got to get him or this whole thing'll start up somewhere else, whether or not you testify."

"Oh no, it won't!" I shouted back. "I know exactly where to find him. But we need to be on the lower floor. We have to get back to the elevator."

"That'll take too long!" said Wren.

But Johnny pointed to a door in the wall. "Darcus's own private staircase is over there! Leads straight down!"

I grinned. We'd got him.

• • •

We were there in under a minute, Wren and me ahead of the others. Wren stepped over the remains of the broken wall and ducked through the arched doorway, an MP5 in his hand.

"Freeze!" he shouted. Then, "What the hell is this?"

"It's a temple," I said. "Don't ask."

Wren whistled. "Cooee, lookee here! We're in a chemical cooker! This place is incredible!" He sniffed. "Still stinks." He cocked the MP5 casually at Darcus. "Don't move."

Darcus was on his knees near the flame, taking something from a shelf beneath it. Rachel was beside him. He put his hand behind his back like a naughty schoolboy caught stealing.

"What's with the flame?" said Wren out of the corner of his mouth.

"When the flame dies, so does the fight," I said.

Wren raised his eyebrows. "OK," he said, and blasted a hole through the back wall, taking the flame with it.

Rachel flattened herself against the wall, her lovely face streaked with tears, her hands shaking.

"I'm glad it's all over!" she sobbed. "I hated it!" She ran forward, her hands out in front. "Take me away!"

Wren pushed her gently aside. "Just get yourself outside for now," he said, putting his MP5 down and checking through one of the cabinets for weapons. "There are people up there who can help you."

Her eyes glistened. "Thank you," she whispered, and slipped out. A second later Java ran in.

She looked around wildly. "Where's Rachel?"

In the center of the oven Darcus lowered himself to the floor, put his head into his hands, and wept.

"You must have seen her," I said. "She went out just before you came in."

"No, she didn't," said Java. She frowned. "You fool, you've let her go!"

Wren spun around. "Guys? Where's my gun?"

Darcus made a gurgling noise. He'd got his head up again now, his face wet with tears. But he wasn't crying, he was laughing.

"*He* knows," shouted Java bitterly. She rounded on me. "I knew right from the start she was a phony, but you wouldn't listen!"

A cold feeling swept over me.

Darcus wiped his eyes and beat his thin chest. "Rachel fooled you all, didn't she?" He burst out laughing again, and by the look on Wren's face, the same unpleasant thought had just struck him.

"Oh yes, my friends," said Darcus, choking with laughter. "She's the brains behind the fight now, not me. It hasn't been me since she was sixteen. I spawned pure evil in her." He stopped and gasped for breath. "You'll never catch her, and she'll just start the whole thing up again."

Wren swore and stamped toward a small door, half-hidden behind a cabinet. It was locked. Rachel must have slipped out through it. "Don't bank on us not catching her," he said.

But Darcus laughed again and said, "But you won't. We're all dead. I gave Rachel her chance. I did that for her. And now at least she'll know that I gave my life to save her and the fight." He beamed his death grin. "Not that she'll care."

Out of nowhere he flourished a remote control.

Wren turned around. "If you've got automatic doors down here, it won't stop us. Phoenix can get through anything, even steel plate." He tapped the cannon on my shoulder.

"No," I said, but I could hardly get my voice out. I could hardly breathe. My worst nightmare was about to come true. "It's not that. It's worse. He's got the place booby-trapped." I looked at Darcus. "You press that button and you die, too."

Darcus walked toward us, holding on to the remote. "Without the fight I'm dead, anyway. This is all that keeps me from being dust and ashes. The energy, the violence, I feed on it. Now it's gone." And he pointed the remote at a black box on the wall and pressed the button.

‖‖ ‖‖ ‖‖ ‖‖ ‖‖ ‖‖ ‖‖ ‖‖ |

A hot wind scorched my face. Then from all around came a dull thud, like a massive heartbeat. The door exploded inward and we were flung across the temple. Banshee howls broke out all around us.

"Perimeter bombs," I yelled to Wren. "We can't get out that way!" And I aimed the cannon at the small door. It vanished. And I hit the wall behind me.

"It's got a bit of a kick, should have warned you!" said Wren. He clamped a cigar between his teeth. "OK, let's go!" He grabbed Ant and tucked him under his arm.

"The ghosts are coming!" said Ant, his hands over his ears.

"No ghosts," said Wren. "It's the iron pillars breaking down and the bomb blast whistling through cracks."

He pulled Java with him, followed by a crocodile line of Rats, and they all disappeared through the smoking hole. I hoisted Johnny to his feet.

"Hang on to me!"

Around us the walls trembled and the floor shook. And as we dragged ourselves to the doorway the bombs went off one by one, in sequence, closer and closer, and our ears popped and the wind burned our skin and the banshees howled around us.

"Move!" I said to Darcus, but he just looked at me with his deathly smile and dropped to his knees.

We flung ourselves through the door hole as another blast ripped through the temple, crushing it as though it was made of tinfoil and sending shrapnel flying into our backs like little daggers.

I looked back as we left and saw Darcus still kneeling, hands raised as if in prayer, but to what god he was praying I couldn't guess. He was covered with brick dust and white as a ghost.

Then the roof came thundering down and he was gone.

◆ ◆ ◆

We ran inside a pipe six feet high and coursing with water, part of the sewers beneath the town. I knew them well; one winter, when nothing much was happening and I wanted to feel the fear, I'd taken to climbing down manholes and running through the pipes below. Until my mammy had found out and thrashed me.

In front of us the shadows of Wren, Java, and the Rats fled. I got my arm firmly around Johnny. He looked up and gave me a serious smile.

"I heard that with Gypsies it was every man for himself."

"You heard wrong," I said, and began dragging him along.

Behind us the labyrinth exploded. Flames licked down the pipe, scorching our backs. Johnny's breath wheezed and whistled in my ear as I dragged him along. And as we fled I ran my hands across the wall. Every hundred feet I knew there was an inspection chamber, where the ladders led up to the manholes.

"A bit farther! Keep going!" I bellowed, until my hand touched empty space. We'd found the chamber. I sneezed.

Then Java's voice said to me, "Freddy, we're in here. Right?" And I froze.

It wasn't my reptile senses this time, just good old human ones. Something was wrong. She hadn't screamed at us, or used the word *idiot* or *oaf*, or cursed me for taking a long time. She hadn't called me Freedom, as she usually did, she hadn't called me Fred. Nobody ever called me Freddy. It was a subtle warning. I sneezed again.

Someone in there with Java knew me, but not well enough to know I wasn't called Freddy as a nickname. And whoever it was had a gun that was making me sneeze. I was betting it was an MP5 held in Rachel's manicured hands.

"OK," I shouted back. "Johnny's in a bad way, I'm having to carry him."

Java's voice had come from the left. The chances were that Rachel was holding her prisoner. So I ran through the doorway and leaped to the left.

I was wrong. Cold steel touched my neck. In front of me Java rolled her eyes. "I said *right! Meaning she's on the right!*"

And Wren beside her said, "Think next time, boy," in a sarcastic way.

"There won't be a next time. You blew it," said Rachel, stepping out of the shadows. "I bet you thought you'd cheated death! Shame."

卌 卌 卌
卌 卌 卌
卌 卌 ||

Guns change everything. Half a second, that's all she needed.

"You're all dead," she said. And smiled her beautiful smile. So this was her love, the thing she lived for. Violence, bloodshed, just like her daddy.

"Keep still," Wren said to me. The tone in his voice was clear. *Don't do anything, leave it to me.* But he was too far away. If anyone was going to get the gun, it had to be me. I was standing right next to her.

"Darcus didn't run that place, you did," I said. Keep her talking, keep her boasting.

Rachel smiled like a goddess of vengeance. "Absolutely right," she said. "But unfortunately you've just signed your own death warrant by being so clever. You're the only ones who know. So if I get rid of you, I'm safe." She aimed the gun. "Think of it like this. Everyone's got to die someday. I'm just sending you to your maker a little early, that's all."

I sneezed.

"Stay still!" she warned.

"Cool it!" I said. "I'm allergic to the gun oil, that's all."

Rachel laughed. "Are you kidding?"

Half a second, that's all it took to squeeze a trigger.

But there might be time enough. Because although it takes half a second to squeeze a trigger, and no one, not even me, has reflexes fast enough to beat a finger squeezing a trigger, there is still time. Fight time. Where your brain works so fast that even a split second is enough to give you the edge.

However bloodthirsty and psycho Rachel was, however much she wanted to shoot us, she still had to make the decision to fire. She had to go from being the gun holder to the one ordering her finger to pull the trigger. When I moved, Rachel's brain had to go through this process. It gave me an extra second for my first move. If it didn't work, I would be dead.

Fight time: one second.

Grab the gun, that's what your brain tells you. *Grab it, push her hand away, take control.* I didn't listen to my brain. Grabbing a hand that's holding a gun is suicide. It takes fine motor skills to grab at a wrist or a forearm quickly enough, and believe me, fine motor skills are at a premium in moments like this. And what about when you've grabbed the hand? It means you're there in front of the gun, right in her line of fire as you struggle to thrust her hand away.

I didn't grab her hand. I sneezed again. It didn't alarm her; she'd heard me sneeze before.

One second. She never even had a chance to see my

forearm coming. It smashed down on her wrist, right on the radial nerve. Her gun hand swung down, the gun clattering to the floor. And I could have carried the move on through, because her head had spun around and I could easily have chopped with the side of my hand and brought her down. But I hesitated, and it gave her just enough time to spin and dive for the gun a fraction of a second before I followed her.

And that's how we ended up with her holding the gun and me throwing myself forward and clasping my hands over hers, so that we were *both* holding the gun, but her fingers were on the trigger and the barrel was pointing right at my chest, and the world hung in the balance and time seemed to stop.

Then, as if in slow motion, I felt her fingers squeeze the trigger. That bullet was going to come out straight into my chest at point-blank range, but there was no worry for me because I was stronger. All I had to do was push the gun to the left. But I couldn't because the gun'd end up pointing at her, and she'd get the bullet. There was the problem. If I pushed it to the right, so it aimed at the wall, I was risking a shot through my own heart on the way. . . .

I didn't even think about it. I took the second route, the one more dangerous for me. The bullet skimmed my chest like a red-hot knife, then hit the wall. And Wren made a noise in his throat and dived across the room like a soccer player.

And the good guy in me sang out and said, *There you are, Fredboy, even when you're right on the edge you still pull out of reptile thinking and do the right thing. You didn't push Clunk into the path of the bus. And to hell with anyone who doesn't believe you.*

My knees buckled. A few seconds' worth of action and I could hardly stand.

Wren had got Rachel against the wall, her hands restrained behind her back. So I picked the gun up and sneezed, and there was a pain in my chest where the bullet had taken a shortcut through me. My ears were starting to sing, and black spots were forming in front of my eyes. It felt like there was a dark wave poised above me.

ＪＨＴ ＪＨＴ ＪＨＴ
ＪＨＴ ＪＨＴ ＪＨＴ
ＪＨＴ ＪＨＴ ＩＩＩ

"Christ! I thought she'd shot you!" said Java.

We came out of the manhole close to Mrs. Bunn's: Java and me elevatoring Johnny out, Wren dragging Rachel with him. And then the Rats emerged, blinking into the light of the day and looking around as if they'd escaped from prison.

Rachel looked over at me, and her beautiful face was quite serene. "You haven't seen the last of me," she said sweetly. A policeman pushed her head down and she got into the back of a police car.

"Don't listen to a word she says," shouted Wren to the driver. "Get her back to the station and stick her in a cell. I'll be back soon."

Surrounding our trailers were police cars, fire engines, and riot vans, and for once it didn't have anything to do with us. Fighters and punters were being lined up and then packed into prisoner transporters. The factory building was ablaze with light, smoke trailing from its windows and the banshees howling from the endless tunnels collapsing beneath it. And clapping and cheering in front of it were the boys who'd helped the police, celebrating their freedom for the first time in their lives.

I pulled at Wren's arm. "I've got to show you something."

Java stopped me. "You need to lie down."

"No, in a moment," I said. The dark wave was still there, but triumph was keeping me upright. I put my hand against my stomach. My T-shirt was soaked with blood, but it could wait. I had one last thing to show to Wren.

"In the café!" I gasped, leading the way. We went up Mrs. Bunn's stairs, my legs like rubber now. I had to hold each one and guide them up the last few steps as though I were a puppet on a string.

Wren gave me a worried look. "Listen, kid, I think you need to lie down," he said, like Java, and then, "For God's sake! How the devil did –?"

And I caught a flash frame of a man lying in bed, surrounded by flowers and a little altar with statues of angels on it.

"Gabby!" said Wren, and his voice broke. "For Christ's sake, man! Where've you been?"

And he began shouting into his cell phone again.

Whoa. Legs very rubbery now. The world was starting to strobe.

Java went to hug me, but then looked at my chest in horror and began to shout for help. And then Wren appeared like a giant, looming over me and shouting into his cell phone for paramedics.

"Catch him, he's going," he said, and the last thing I saw before the dark wave crashed over me was Java crying.

Or maybe I dreamed that part.

I came to in a hospital.

There were three beds in the room. Johnny was next to me, lying back with his eyes closed and earphones over his head, and playing air guitar very gingerly. The bed opposite was occupied by the man I'd last seen in Mrs. Bunn's bedroom. He was propped up eating a knickerbocker glory and watching the small TV on his bedside table.

In the corridor outside a woman pushed a tea trolley by, a sniper rifle slung over her shoulder. I closed my eyes. Perhaps I hadn't fully come to yet. A moment later I opened them again, and a young girl ran by and glanced in. She smiled at me and winked, which was cute except she had a green tint to her skin and hair, and vivid green eyes.

"Hey, come here!" I said, but she smiled and ran off.

Johnny strummed a last chord and saw that I was awake. He gave me his serious smile. "Thanks, man, for getting me out."

"That's OK." I kept my eye on the door. "So is it back to school and exams now?" I said.

He laughed. "Me? My father has spent tens of thousands on my education, and I failed every single test last year. Java's the one with the brains."

A nurse walked in. Her white uniform was nothing out of the ordinary, but the handcuffs in her pocket weren't National Health issue.

"No talking!" she snapped.

She stomped over to the bloke opposite and put a thermometer in his mouth, glancing at her watch. "Remember anything yet?" she snapped.

"No," he said.

She stomped out. The bloke winked at us.

I narrowed my eyes. "What sort of hospital is this?" I muttered.

I looked out the window. Stretching away outside was the sort of garden you'd see around a palace, with fountains and bushes in the shape of peacocks. Beyond the garden, things got very strange. There was what looked like an assault course. And over to the left a firing range. As I watched, there was a distant boom and one of the targets disappeared in a puff of smoke.

One thing was for sure, I wasn't in the Royal Infirmary in the center of town.

"This place is Phoenix, isn't it?" I said.

Johnny looked at me with shining eyes. "Yes! And I know exactly what I want to do with my life now. I'm going to join them."

He smiled like he'd seen the light. He had another

belief to follow now. Jeez, maybe one day he'd use his power for himself, not give it away to someone else.

I yawned. I'd still got a few nights' worth of sleep to catch up on.

When I opened my eyes, Johnny was asleep and another cop was walking by the ward door. "Hey, Gabby! Get the hell out of that bed," he shouted. "The Lizardman case has just come on the board!"

The bloke stared at him blankly, then went back to his TV.

I had to get out of here. I looked around for my clothes, but I found Java instead. Sitting in the chair next to my bed, reading a book.

"I need my jeans," I said.

She blew a gum bubble and ignored what I'd just said, as usual. "Do you want anything to eat?" she said eventually.

Food! Now there was a thought. I lay back on my pillow. "Bacon, crispy, the fat trimmed off, eggs flipped over, coffee, and a bagel, please."

Java looked down at her lap. "I've got a KitKat or a Kraft cheese slice. The trolley didn't have much."

"OK. Then I'll have some clothes instead. Pants, jeans, track bottoms, anything'll do," I said. "I'm getting out of here."

By the way, did I say Java was now holding my hand? She was. Neither of us said anything about it, but that's how it was. Don't read anything into it, it was part of the day we'd had. After what we'd been through she probably knew me better than anyone else in the world, which was a freaky thing since I'd only known her a few days. So maybe a little hand-holding was in order. It wasn't like we were ever going to see each other again after today. I'd be back on the road, and she'd be back in a school uniform doing sums in a classroom. "World A" and "World B," don't forget. There was her reality and then there was mine.

I watched her for a minute.

"Jeez, girl, you were brave, going into that place to find Johnny."

"I wasn't, I was scared to death," she said. "It was worse than when Lucifer came for me."

I looked at her blankly. "Oh right, Lucifer." Just for a while there I'd forgotten she was crazy.

She saw the look on my face. "My father's guard dog, Lucifer, OK?" she continued. "It attacked me one night. I'd never been so scared until now."

I laughed. It felt like the first time I'd laughed in years; I swear my face had forgotten how to do it. We looked at each other for a moment.

"You were brave. You can't be brave unless you're scared," I said. "I'd say that you're now an honorary Gypsy, and that's high praise."

She inclined her head like a princess receiving a bouquet. "Thank you. Your sister and the little girls are coming to see you soon," she said. "We're miles out in the countryside, so they're camping in the parking lot until you get released. The boss of Phoenix is complaining like mad, but Crystal says she's not budging." Java was still holding my hand, but fiddling with something on the floor. It turned out to be the backpack, bulging softly. "By the way, this is yours," she said, and kicked it under the bed.

"The reward money?"

She nodded.

"You'll need to take it back, now that you're going back home," I said.

"Nope," she said, in that vexing way. "It'll make no difference, and you deserve it. And my father will never know you have it, I promise." She looked me in the eye. "You saved my life. Trust me, no one will ever know where that money went." She kicked the backpack a little farther under the bed. "Oh, and I lied about the amount. I was going to use the rest of the money I stole to start a new life for me and Johnny, but running away isn't the answer."

"You going back to school now?" I said, trying to see whether I could sit up properly without making her let go of my hand.

She shook her head. "I've been expelled. My dad's talking about sending me to a private school on Gozo."

"Gozo?"

"A little island next to Malta. In the middle of the Mediterranean, far away from bad influences."

See what I mean? It looked like we weren't even going to be in the same country. And then she got up and perched on the bed at the side of me and held my hand with both of hers, and all I can say is I'm glad I wasn't rigged up to one of those heart monitors that bleep.

"But it's fine," she said, and squeezed my hand. "It's all going to work out."

"Did your mammy tell you?" I said.

She shook her head. "No, Mum's moved on. It's someone called Lone Wolf; he says he's my spirit guide now," she said. "He's much better about the future than Mum." She raised her eyebrows. "Well, mine and yours, anyway."

Lone Wolf? The girl *was* crazy. I tried sitting up a bit more.

"So what's Lone Wolf been telling you?"

She looked down at me and gave me the pixie smile again. "Oh, lots of stuff," she said, and laughed to herself.

"What?" I said, my head beginning to swim.

"Wait and see."

I lay back. Who knows, maybe Lone Wolf knew a thing or two about "Worlds A" and "B," and maybe we could get together and make "World C," where who you were and how much money you had didn't matter that much.

A woman cop appeared at the door this time. "Time's up," she said to Java.

273

Java gave me a sad smile. "Got to go and be charged with theft."

"But—" I began. But Java leaned over and kissed me quickly. "It's going to be all right – Lone Wolf told me," she whispered, and was gone.

My eyes began to close.

The next thing I remember is something touching my arm.

Sweet Mercy! Two spaniel eyes atop a pair of jimjams, like the ghost of some poor Victorian street urchin. "For Christ's sake, kid! Do you have to creep up on me like that?"

"Soz," said Ant, but I could see there was something bothering him. "They gived me a bath!" he complained. "And throwed my commando pants away. And I can't have candy. Because I've got to look after my teeth!"

I leaned over, winced, and hurriedly sat up again. "Get *me* some pants, Ant, anything. See if you can find the store where they keep the surgeons' outfits."

He didn't budge. "Can I stay with you?" he said. I don't know whether he meant just for now or forever, but I nodded. Maybe he was capable of hypnosis, because my eyes began to droop again.

"Sit in that chair, if you want," I said. "I'm just going to have five minutes' kip, and then you can get my clothes."

Ant curled up in the armchair by the bed. I closed my eyes and opened them, and he was fast asleep, and Wren was sprawled in the other chair, his legs halfway across the ward, texting on his phone.

I'd had it with all this falling asleep. I had to get out of here.

"Did Java get me some pants?" I said. Wren looked up and shook his head.

"Where's she gone?" I said. I managed to get myself into a sitting position and swing my legs around. They'd got me in a nightie or something. The sooner I got out of this hellhole the better.

Wren watched me with his eyes narrowed, crunching away on a mouthful of Tic Tacs – cigars must not be allowed in hospitals. "She's answering some serious questions downstairs, about the fifty thousand pounds missing from her father's company."

That stopped me in my tracks. "Five thousand, you mean."

"No, fifty thousand. She says she lost it when she was living rough. Boy, has that young lady got a lot of explaining to do."

I swear, it seemed like the backpack beneath my bed had started beeping and flashing.

"Java Sparrow," I said, shaking my head in admiration. "Master criminal."

"Quite something, huh?" said Wren. A few small creases appeared around his eyes, probably indicating he was smiling. "But I'd say that any girl who dares to follow you into a den of killers shouldn't have much trouble persuading a few cops she's just a mixed-up rich kid who's made a little mistake."

"What happened to Leon?"

Wren shook his head. "He didn't make it out. He was probably doomed, anyway. Gene-splicing and cloning don't work at the moment, even for Darcus. The human body can't take it and things start to mutate."

No sooner had I met my one and only brother than he'd gone again. I would've liked to see if we could've mended him.

"Will he get a funeral?" Smith funerals were something to behold. We kept the tradition where we burned the trailer after someone died, to free their spirit.

"One of our medics saw him lying in the pit, not moving. But then the bomb blast set fire to the place. We never got him out."

So maybe he did get a real Gypsy funeral, after all. Now I was left with seven sisters again.

"I don't suppose he could have escaped?" I said.

Again Wren shook his head. "No mortal man could have survived that inferno."

I let it go. It was for the best.

I tried to stand up. Every muscle in my body complained, but at least I was getting somewhere now. I reached under the bed for the backpack. I tested it for weight; it was heavy. I knew what five grand in bills felt like, and it didn't feel like this. Maybe Crystal would get her land after all. Then I had another go at standing up. I grabbed the drip stand for support.

"Wren, about this Hercules gene," I said. Something had been on my mind for a while now. "How can I find out what happened to old Hercules? All we know is that he disappeared one day, after he was sentenced to be hanged. I need to find out if he turned into a monster." I took a deep breath. "And if I'm going to turn into one, too, like Leon."

Wren made a barking noise. It might have been a laugh. "Hercules a monster? Not that I heard! He worked for us for many years, and then when things got too hot, we made him disappear." Wren leaned back in his chair. "Hercules was no monster, he was one of our best men."

I held on to the drip stand and stared blankly at Wren. "Hercules worked for Phoenix? Wren, stop messing around. Did they even have cops in the 1850s?"

"There were police, but he was in Phoenix. We've been around a very, very long time." Wren sat forward and gave me his cop's stare. "The people who run this world make sure that most of you know very little about what's really going on. But believe me, boy, reality is stranger than you could ever imagine. When you work for Phoenix, you begin to see the world as it really is."

"So maybe there is a place in the world for a freak like me," I said.

Wren nodded. "You did all right back there. Came to

your senses, did the right thing," he said, getting his huge feet out of the way as I used the drip stand to take a few tottering steps.

"Thanks," I said casually.

"And finding Gabby was the cherry on the cake," he continued as I limped by. "You were right. He gave himself away after Darcus got him with a truth drug. He managed to get himself out of the Bear Pit and through the crawl space, and then collapsed in Mrs. Bunn's cellar. She found him, thought he was the archangel Gabriel, and tended him from then onward. He's got amnesia." He glanced across at Gabby, who was still watching TV with the thermometer in his mouth. "Can't remember a thing yet, but he's hooked on knickerbocker glories."

He paused, and I knew there was more.

"Not a bad job you did there," he said, and unhooked the chart from the end of the bed, peeled a little sticky gold star from a sheet of paper, and stuck it on the front of my gown. "You are now officially a Phoenix probationary. Of course, if you're going to work for us again, you're going to have to get some discipline –"

I stopped him right there. "I don't work for anyone, Wren," I said. I continued on up the ward, but I was hardly escaping at hyperspeed. He caught me up and held my elbow to help me along.

"Want any help with that backpack?" The gold tooth glinted for a moment.

"No," I said.

"Thought not," he said. We continued walking slowly.

"I wouldn't employ you as you are," he said as we made our way up the ward. "You lack the control that's needed in these situations. But there's a training course we do here at Phoenix HQ; it's advanced undercover stuff."

I'd have laughed, but it hurt too much.

"No chance," I said. Then I leaned on his arm, trying not to bend and set my stitches throbbing. "But if you could get me my jeans and something to cover this bandage, then I could get myself out of here."

"Can't do it, you need the rest," he said.

"I've had all the rest I can take. Seriously, just get me out of here," I said. "I can't stand hospitals."

Wren shook his head. "Can't do it," he said again. "They want you in overnight, to keep an eye on you."

I was nearly at the door. "I swear I'll go crazy, you've got to get my clothes so I can make a break for it."

Wren folded his arms, blocking the doorway. "Sorry, lad. I've no jurisdiction. I'm not a relative, and you're not one of my men."

I was desperate, you understand, or I would never have said it. I took a deep breath.

"What if I worked for you, would you get me out of here then?"

A few more creases appeared beside Wren's eyes.

"Now that's a different story."